Bullets crashed into Gary Manning's chest

The impact hurled the Phoenix Force vet backward into a wall. Stunned by the throbbing pain in his chest, he slid to the floor. As he was going down, he saw Encizo double up and fall beside him.

The combat-hardened warrior tried to raise his AK-47, but a black-booted figure stepped forward and stamped a heel on the rifle, pinning it to the floor.

The terrorist crouched beside the stricken Manning and aimed a Russian Makarov pistol at his head.

"Bang, bang, American," he mocked in heavily accented English. "You are dead!"

Mack Bolan's
PHOENIX FORCE

Mack Bolan's
ABLE TEAM

PHOENIX FORCE

Harvest Hell

Gar Wilson

A GOLD EAGLE BOOK FROM

W🦅RLDWIDE

TORONTO • NEW YORK • LONDON • PARIS
AMSTERDAM • STOCKHOLM • HAMBURG
ATHENS • MILAN • TOKYO • SYDNEY

First edition September 1984

ISBN 0-373-61313-X

Special thanks and acknowledgment to
William Fieldhouse for his contributions to this work.

1

A man shouldn't have to die in an antiseptic cell, Colonel Yakov Katzenelenbogen thought. Especially not a man like Uri Yosefthal. God knows, he has suffered enough.

Katz stood looking down on a white hospital bed. Beneath stiff white sheets lay a shriveled old man. His bulblike head rested on a white pillow as he stared up at the ceiling. His wrinkled pale face seemed determined to blend with its surroundings. Katz almost expected to see the old man fade into the white decor. Into oblivion.

So much had happened since Katz and Uri Yosefthal had first met, since that day in 1946 when Katz, an eighteen-year-old veteran of the Resistance in France, had encountered an equally youthful Yosefthal.

Owing to his fluency with languages and his undercover work for the American OSS, Katz had landed a job with the U.S. Army as a translator. That was how he met the wasted figure who now lay before him.

Uri Yosefthal was a survivor of Hitler's Dachau death camp, and Katz was stunned by the irony that the first time he'd set eyes on Uri, the young refugee had been a scrawny stick figure with hollow cheeks, rotten teeth and soft bones—looking not much different from what he did now. But back then, Uri's eyes had been bright and fierce, his mind alert and keen.

Uri Yosefthal had stood defiantly in front of Katz that day in 1946 and told him he wanted to be sent to Russia. Katz had tried to persuade him to abandon such a foolish idea. Did he not know that Stalin was no better than Hitler? Had he not suffered enough?

Three and a half decades later, Katz himself was a wounded but proud warrior. But the wounds were deep and permanent. Both his wife and son were dead, victims of a violent world. Katz himself had lost his right forearm and hand in the Six Day War. They had been replaced with a remarkable prosthesis that featured interchangeable parts, including a single-shot .22 pistol in the index finger. He had served in the Hagannah and the Mossad and worked with the CIA. Now he was the unit commander of Phoenix Force, the crack antiterrorist unit that had been brought together by Colonel John Phoenix— better known as Mack Bolan, or the Executioner.

But not even Phoenix Force could save Uri Yosefthal, Katz thought as he stared down at the dry, white-parchment skin that was stretched over the bones of Yosefthal's face. He thought of how the youthful refugee had become a freedom fighter within the Soviet Union. Officially labeled a dissident, Yosefthal had been tried for treason and sent to a Siberian forced-labor camp. In the West his heroism had led to many appeals for his release. All had been denied. Until now.

Without any notice, Uri Yosefthal was exiled to the United States.

The shriveled figure stirred on the hospital bed.

"Uri?" Yakov said softly. "Can you hear me?"

"Yakov?" came the reply as recognition floated across Yosefthal's rheumy eyes. "It has been a long time."

"A hundred years ago," Katz replied.

"So it seems," Yosefthal said. "You were right about many things, my friend. I should have gone with you to Palestine."

"Not all the dreams about Israel came true, Uri," Katz told him. "Neither of us found Utopia."

"Do you think it exists?"

"I hope not." The Israeli grinned. "It would probably bore me to death."

"Still a warrior, eh?" Yosefthal chuckled harshly. "I suspected you would not change. I always assumed you'd be dead by now."

"I came close to it a couple of times," Katz admitted.

"I came closer," Yosefthal said bitterly. "How did you know I was here?"

"We've been interested in you for a long time, Uri."

" 'We' ?" Yosefthal raised his white eyebrows. "Do you mean the Israelis or the Americans?"

"Both," Katz answered. "We tried to negotiate your release. The Americans wanted to trade two KGB spies for your freedom. Tel Aviv made an appeal to the United Nations to pressure the Soviets to allow you to emigrate to Israel. We were even considering a commando raid...."

"A 'raid'?" Yosefthal laughed hoarsely. "No one could penetrate the Soviet Union and successfully rescue a prisoner from Siberia."

"You'd be surprised what a few good men can do," Katz replied.

"None of that matters now." Yosefthal sighed. "I'm free now. The Kremlin sent me to the United States and I'm going to die in this damned hospital bed."

"Listen, Uri," Katz began. "The Russians gave no reason why they suddenly decided to release you. But you've been ill since you arrived in the United States, and our doctors haven't been able to determine what's wrong with you."

"You think the KGB gave me some sort of exotic poison?" Yosefthal remarked. "The American Naval doctors would have detected that. The simple fact is, I'm dying of malnutrition. Ironic, isn't it? I survived a diet of gruel, boiled grass and fish heads in a labor camp, but I can no longer digest food here in the United States."

"It doesn't make sense, Uri."

"It is fate, Yakov," Yosefthal stated. "I'm really not afraid of dying, you know. Most of my life has been spent struggling for freedom. For myself and for others. Now I realize freedom is an illusion. Only the dead are truly free."

"Would you like to talk to a rabbi?" Katz inquired.

"No," Yosefthal replied. "I do not need anyone's help to pray. If God is not willing to accept my soul, no words from a rabbi will change His mind."

"You might find some comfort in a reading from the Torah."

"I would find comfort in seeing the sky and breathing air that does not smell like medicine. I would like to smell flowers and hear birds singing. I would rather die under the sun than in this tomb.''

"There's a garden outside." Katz smiled. "Plenty of carnations, roses and other flowers there.''

"Will they let me leave?" Yosefthal asked.

"Why tell them we're leaving?" Katz shrugged.

He gazed down at Yosefthal. A second ago, the specter of a smile had started to wash over his face; now Yosefthal's eyes stared up at the ceiling without blinking. Katz placed two fingers to the side of the Russian dissident's neck and felt for a pulse. There was none.

"Good bye, Uri," Katz whispered hoarsely. "Your ordeal is finally over."

He put his fingertips on the dead man's eyelids and gently pushed them shut.

2

"I'm sorry about your friend, Yakov," Hal Brognola said as he handed Katz a cup of coffee.

"Uri wasn't exactly a 'friend,'" Katzenelenbogen replied, nodding his thanks. "But in his own way, he was fighting the same enemy as the rest of us."

"He died of malnutrition?" Brognola frowned. He sank into a chair at the head of a walnut conference table. "That hardly seems possible. Didn't the Navy medical team confirm that Yosefthal was healthy? Christ, they even had a nutritionist supervise his meals."

"Nobody has any idea what was wrong with Uri," the Phoenix Force head honcho stated. "An autopsy confirmed he couldn't digest food. That's all anyone knows for sure." Katz used the steel hook at the end of his prosthesis to tear open a pack of Camel cigarettes. "But you didn't call me here to discuss Uri Yosefthal."

"No," Brognola admitted. "I didn't."

Hal Brognola was the control officer of all Stony Man operations. He had the monumental task of go-between for the President of the United States and the unique top-secret organization. The Stony Man operations complex had been created by Mack Bolan and the President of the United States to combat international terrorism. Phoenix Force was under the Stony Man umbrella.

Stony Man was unlike most other covert organizations because it was not designed to handle general intelligence gathering or personnel investigations. The CIA, FBI, Interpol and other agencies unknowingly provided this kind of data. Stony Man had only two concerns: *locate problems and terminate them by whatever methods necessary to get the job done*. Thus far, Stony Man's success rate had been one hundred percent.

Yet the price for victory can often be high. Stony Man had suffered several losses, and recent tragic events had shaken the very foundation of the organization.

The Stony Man fortress was attacked, betrayed by a highly placed mole in the President's circle. Andrzej Konzaki, the resident armorer and weapons authority, had been killed. Aaron Kurtzman, the warriors' computer wizard, was badly wounded, confined to a wheelchair, crippled for life.

The enemy soon regretted the murderous siege. Mack Bolan had retaliated with a vengeance, and the terrorists paid in blood. But war is a double-edged sword, and the Executioner's woman, April Rose, became another casualty.

For Stony Man the ordeal had just begun.

The organization had practically been built around one man—the Executioner. But when Bolan was framed for a political assassination by the Soviet KGB, he became a renegade wanted by every intelligence and law-enforcement network in the world. He was no longer part of Stony Man. Not even Brognola or the President could help Bolan now.

The future of Stony Man was uncertain following this incredible upset. However, a sinister terrorist plot within the United States required immediate action. The sort of action only Stony Man was equipped to handle. Phoenix Force had been assigned the task.

Once again the price of victory was paid for with blood. Keio Ohara, one of the original five members of Phoenix Force, was killed during the final battle with the Black Alchemist terrorists.

The newest member of the team, Calvin James, had done well on the last mission. Since then James had been spending the past two months undergoing grueling training with the other men of Phoenix Force to ensure that the unit would perform smoothly as a team. Brognola was confident Phoenix Force was ready for their next assignment.

"We've got a job for you guys," Brognola began as he slid a buff file folder across the table to Katz. "Kurtzman put that together less than an hour ago. Most of the information and photographs are from our European connections with Interpol. Kurtzman cross-checked with the CIA, BND, SIS—everybody short of the Boy Scouts of America—to make sure everything is accurate."

Katz smiled. "I take it our mission will be in Europe?"

"In Greece, to be exact," the fed began, unwrapping a cigar. "Open that thing up and take a look at who's vacationing there this year."

Katz opened the folder and gazed down at the photograph of a middle-aged man dressed in a beige lightweight suit with a white shirt open at the throat. A pair of cheap sunglasses were perched on the bridge of his nose. His dark-gray hair was combed straight back from a high forehead.

The man could have been a bank teller or a grocery-store manager from any country on the face of the earth. He looked like a tourist. He was the sort of man no one would notice in a crowd. The type perfectly suited for clandestine operations.

Katz turned over the photograph and read the man's file:

SUBJECT IDENTIFICATION CONFIRMED
Name: Kostov, Nikolai Ivanovich
Nationality: People's Republic of Bulgaria
Occupation: Colonel, Bulgarian Security Service
Misc. Info: Kostov first came to our attention during World War II. He was part of the Red Lions commando underground, a Communist group that fought the Nazis in Greece. Kostov served with valor. Awarded the Gold Star of the Heroes of the People's Republic of Bulgaria, the highest military decoration awarded in that country. Kostov speaks Bulgarian, Russian, Greek and English fluently, and some German and Turkish. He has received special training in the USSR. No details available, but we know Kostov is currently attached to the KGB's Department Eleven in Sofia, Bulgaria.

From 1971 to 1974 he served with the Bulgarian embassy in Greece. No evidence of espionage activity at that time. Unconfirmed possibility that Kostov was involved in the conspiracy to assassinate Pope John-Paul II. May have helped transport Mehmet Ali Agca from Turkey to Bulgaria and later to Yugoslavia and eventually Italy. No other details available.

"This is all you have on Kostov?" the Israeli colonel inquired.

"That's it," Brognola answered, lighting his cigar. "All we know is he's a high mucky-muck in the Bulgarian secret police and that he's currently staying on an island off the coast of Greece."

"I agree it's reason for concern," Katz began. "This Kostov must be good. He's kept a low profile for the past forty years. He's good at keeping his secrets secret. Still, this looks like a problem for the Greek authorities and the regular intelligence networks of the free world. It doesn't seem to be the sort of thing that would usually involve Phoenix Force."

"Keep reading the file," Brognola told him.

Katz opened the folder again and found another photograph. A young blond man with icy blue eyes stared back at him. Heinrich Himmler would have loved the guy, Katz thought. He looked like an advertisement for rent-an-Aryan.

"Captain Igor Vitosho," Katz remarked as he scanned over the next file report. "There's a lot more on this character than Kurtzman found on Kostov."

"You can read it later," the fed stated. "There's a lot of information on the guy, but it won't really help much. Vitosho is a commando in the Bulgarian parachute corps. Received advanced training from an elite Russian paratrooper outfit."

"The Vozdushno Desantnye Vojska?" Katz asked.

"Beats me." Brognola shrugged. "You speak Russian, not me. Whoever trained Vitosho did a hell of a job. The reason his file is so thick is that he spent sixteen months in Nicaragua training Sandinistan soldiers at a Soviet-built special-forces camp. You'll find several photos of the captain in that folder. He instructed troops in parachuting, small arms, hand-to-hand combat and underwater demolitions. A hard ass."

"An interesting pair," the Israeli mused. "The Bulgarians sent a superspy and a supercommando. I see why you suspect they might be up to espionage or terrorist activity. But Greece isn't South Yemen or Libya. Even if these two are part of the Bulgarian embassy, the Greeks should still be able to deport them as undesirables."

"It isn't that simple, Yakov," Brognola explained. "You see, Kostov and Vitosho are guests on the island of Krio. Understand?"

"Krio?" Katz raised an eyebrow. "That wouldn't happen to be the property of Dimitri Krio, the shipping tycoon, by any chance?"

"Not by chance at all," the Stony Man control replied. "Krio owns that island. Technically, it's his private little country."

"Come on, Hal." Katz sighed. "The Greeks must have the authority to do something about Bulgarian agents stationed on one of their islands."

Brognola looked at the Phoenix Force vet and shrugged. "You know damn good and well that money is power anywhere in the world. The Greek authorities don't want to push Krio because he has friends in the government. Don't tell me that surprises you, Katz.''

"So the Greeks don't want to handle this, and the CIA doesn't want to get involved, either.''

"That's right,'' the fed stated. "But we're not just taking this mission because it's unpopular. Leaf through that shit on Vitosho and tell me what you see.''

The Israeli did as Brognola suggested. He soon found a face he immediately recognized. The swarthy bearded features of Jabari Khatid were displayed in a photograph. Katz leafed through more files and found two more familiar faces.

"Khatid, Gerhart and Shigata,'' the Israeli remarked. "I don't recognize any of the others, but I assume that if former members of Black September, the Baader-Meinhof gang and the Japanese Red Army are on Krio's island, the rest of these jokers must be from similar terrorist organizations.''

"Not many of them are known terrorists,'' Brognola explained. "But most of them have a record for political violence and radical behavior. Assaulting police officers during political demonstrations, destroying public property, stuff like that. Krio has almost a hundred young zealots barracked on his island.''

"Sounds like they're planning something on an international level,'' Katz said grimly.

"That's what we figure, too,'' Brognola agreed. "And that's why we need Phoenix Force.''

"Indeed.'' Katz nodded. "Have you contacted the others?''

"McCarter will meet you in Greece," the fed answered. "But I'm still trying to get in touch with the other three. One thing's for sure—you guys had better be at full strength for this mission. Besides the terrorists and the Bulgarians, Krio also has a security force of twenty-seven men. All are well trained and licensed to carry submachine guns while guarding Krio's island estate."

"Any idea how we should handle this mission?" Katz inquired.

"You seem to work best when I let you play it by ear," Brognola said with a grin.

"In this case," Katz replied, "I don't think we'd object to a little help with the tune."

3

Gary Manning wheeled his Chevy pickup along the rutted dirt road. A tent and miscellaneous camping gear shuffled around in the box back of the cab every time the tires dipped into a hole. Manning hoped everything would stay in the truck. He also hoped he would find a shop soon and it would have a telephone.

Manning hated to terminate a camping trip ahead of schedule. It was his favorite form of relaxation and one he seldom had time to enjoy. He had just been preparing to do some climbing when the pager he wore on his belt had beeped the ominous message that his office had an urgent call for him. With his portable telephone out of order, he'd had no choice but to strike camp and move on.

Basically a loner, Manning had an unquenchable desire to accomplish as much as possible. He possessed an unlimited supply of endurance and determination and was hell-bent on achieving any goal he set.

This incredible drive had always set Gary Manning apart from his peers. As a youth he didn't study subjects in school; he devoured them. He didn't play sports; he made war on his opponents. He had a reputation as a hard-nosed, unrelenting son of a bitch who attacked a task and didn't quit until it was finished.

As a lieutenant in the Canadian army, Manning had served in the corps of engineers where he specialized in explosives and became one of the best demolitions experts in the world. His military career included a tour of duty in Vietnam as an "observer."

He worked with the 5th Special Forces and the clandestine Special Operations Group for more than a year, using his skill with explosives to destroy NVA bases. Manning's prowess with a rifle made him as successful a sniper as he was a deer hunter in the Canadian forests. His exceptional ability and courage did not go unrecognized. Gary Manning was one of the few Canadian citizens to receive the Silver Star from the United States Army for valor.

The Royal Canadian Mounted Police took an interest in Manning, which led to a position with their antiterrorist division, chiefly concerned with the Quebec Liberation Front and Soviet espionage within Canada. The RCMP had been worried about the latter ever since Igor Gouzenko, a Russian embassy clerk, defected in Ottawa in 1945.

Manning had the unique honor of working with the elite GSG-9 antiterrorists in West Germany, thanks to an exchange program between the Germans and the Canadians. Thus Manning had received firsthand experience in urban warfare, as well as jungle combat.

The RCMP was put out of the espionage business after a scandal concerning illegal wiretapping and other abuses of power. However, in 1981, the newly formed Canadian Security Intelligence Service offered Manning an administrative job. Manning refused. He had decided to work for the private sector, marry and raise a family. The marriage soon ended in divorce, but Manning quickly excelled in the business world as a security consultant and a junior executive for North America International.

Then Stony Man contacted the Canadian dynamo and made him an offer to become part of the greatest team of antiterrorists in the history of the world. The offer was more than Gary Manning could resist.

AT LAST Manning located a roadside store. A little wood-frame ma-and-pa place, it was a small general store fronted by a pair of gas pumps that stood in the dust like sentinels and a shiny aluminum telephone booth. The Canadian pulled up to the shop, jumped out and headed for the phone.

He heard the harsh thunder of several motorcycles ripping up the dirt road from the opposite direction but ignored the noise as he extracted coins from a pocket and fed them into the telephone. He dialed the number to his Montreal office. Helen St. Clair, his secretary, answered.

"This is Manning," he told her. "You've got a message for me?"

The rumble of motorcycles became a monstrous roar as four ambassadors of the great unwashed rode up to the store on Harley-Davidson hogs. They pulled up next to the gas pumps and laughed as they rolled their throttles in a contest to see who had the noisiest machine. Manning could barely hear Helen's voice over the bellow of engines.

"Mr. Manning?" she asked, concern in her voice. "Are you all right, sir?"

"No problem," Manning assured her. "Just some kids working on their motor bikes. Will you please repeat that message?"

The bikers suffocated their hogs and dismounted. Manning didn't like the looks of the group. They were dressed in black leather, Levi's and dirt. All wore beards, dark glasses and sneers. Trouble came off them like a bad smell.

"The message was from a Mr. Bascomb," Helen answered. "He said he needs to meet with you about a business deal. Said it was confidential, but that you already know most of it."

"Oh, yeah," Manning replied. "Bascomb works in Washington. Likes to keep a low profile and expects his associates to do likewise."

"Will you be flying to Washington, sir?"

"Guess I'd better," he answered. "Might be gone for a few days again."

"You've been making a lot of trips lately."

"They've all been necessary," Manning declared.

"Should Henderson handle things until you get back?"

"That'll be fine," Manning confirmed as he watched the four motorcycle hoods approach his truck. "I've got a lot to do, Helen. Better get to it. Thanks for everything."

Manning hung up and emerged from the phone booth. Two of the bikers had climbed into the back of the truck and pawed through Manning's camping gear. A wiry, goat-faced character tried to jimmy the door with a metal strip. A husky ape with a Nazi helmet stood in front of the truck and smiled at Manning.

"Well, ain't you a big cheese head," the gorilla

chuckled. "You one of them Canadian lumberjacks? Just lumber over here, Jack. Let's see how tough you are."

The others laughed. No single member of the gang would have dared challenge Manning to a fight. The Canadian indeed resembled a lumberjack. Although less than six feet tall, coils of thick muscles strained against the fabric of his checkered shirt and denim trousers.

Together the bikers had ample courage. They also carried a variety of chains and sheath knives. The Canadian guessed they probably had other concealed weapons, as well. Manning hoped none of them had a gun tucked inside his black leather jacket. The Canadian's .300 Winchester Magnum was locked inside the truck. A .357 snubnose Colt was hidden in a special holster under the front seat. Neither offered much comfort as the unarmed Canadian approached the gang.

"You guys looking for anything special?" Manning asked, strolling toward the ape-man in front of the truck.

"We'll take what we want, cheese head," the hood with the jimmy announced. "And that includes your life, sucker."

Goat face tossed the jimmy aside and drew a Bowie knife from his belt. The husky character reached for a thick steel chain wrapped around his paunchy waist. Manning held up his hands in surrender.

"Hand over your wallet, cheese head," the goat-faced leader ordered. "Or we'll take it off your fuckin' corpse."

"I don't want any trouble," Manning replied, lowering his arms.

Without warning, he lashed out a leg. The gorilla screamed when the steel-capped toe of a boot crashed into his testicles. Manning rushed forward and seized the stunned biker before the ape could free his fighting chain. The Canadian whirled and swung his opponent into goat face, who was about to execute a knife thrust.

The gorilla screamed again when the blade of the Bowie stabbed into his meaty side. Goat face yanked his knife from his partner's flesh, startled by the fact he had wounded one of his own men. Before he could use the Bowie again, Gary Manning chopped the side of a hand across the hood's wrist. The knife fell from numb fingers.

Manning quickly rammed the point of his elbow into the biker's solar plexus. The hoodlum gasped as the wind rushed from his tortured lungs. Another elbow smash hit the man on the point of his bearded chin, and the gang leader crumbled to the ground, unconscious.

Although wounded and suffering considerable pain, the gorilla still made another attempt to free his chain belt. He pawed at the weapon with both hands. This was a mistake, because he did not have time to raise an arm to block the left hook Manning swung into the side of his head. The ape's head bounced when a right uppercut plowed under his jaw. Manning's left fist punched the big man in the left temple. The gorilla went down for keeps.

"Jesus, shit," a biker exclaimed as the two remaining gang members leaped down from the back of the truck.

Manning pivoted to face the pair. One thug had drawn a switchblade. His partner smiled as he held up both arms. The guy wore a pair of leather gauntlets armed with steel studs and spikes, which covered his fists and forearms.

Spikes attacked first. He jabbed a boxer's left fist at Manning, then slashed his right forearm at the Canadian's skull. Manning sidestepped quickly. The steel-studded limb whipped air inches from the Phoenix Force commando. Manning slammed a karate hammer fist to the small of Spikes's back. The motorcycle hood tumbled headlong to the dust, but his knife-wielding partner kept coming.

Manning jumped away from a knife slash. Sharp steel slit his shirt and the cold blade scraped his skin. The Canadian hardly noticed the sting of the minor wound. His attention was centered on the knife artist, who executed a deadly thrust for Manning's throat.

The Canadian dodged the attack and quickly seized the man's arm behind the switchblade. He locked the elbow to apply a straight-arm bar and rammed a knee lift to the biker's abdomen. The knife artist doubled up with a grunt. Before Manning could finish off his opponent, Spikes charged back into the melee and threw a vicious kick for Manning's groin.

The Phoenix Force pro hauled his captive into the path of the second biker's boot. Spikes kicked his partner right in the mouth. Manning immediately lunged forward and drove the knife man's skull into Spikes's chest. The second goon staggered backward from the blow. Manning's captive sagged. The Canadian clubbed him behind the ear with his fist to be certain the man was unconscious before he released the biker.

Only Spikes remained. He rushed Manning and swung a desperate steel-studded fist at the Canadian's face. Manning dodged the cestus, and Spikes lashed a sideways forearm stroke at Manning's head. The commando suddenly dropped to one knee and ducked under the attacking limb.

The Canadian grabbed his opponent's ankles and yanked. Spikes's feet left the ground, and he crashed to earth hard. The man's backbone was still tingling with needles of pain when Manning rose and stamped his boot between Spikes's splayed legs. The biker uttered a single high-pitched shriek and passed out from the tidal wave of agony.

"By God, that was surely some fight, mister!" an old man's reedy voice exclaimed.

Manning turned to see a white-haired, wrinkled figure emerge from the store. The old man held a double-barrel shotgun. He smiled at Manning as he tucked the weapon into the crook of his elbow.

"When I seen the ruckus I loaded my gun," the shop owner declared. "Sorry I took so long. Couldn't recall where I left my bloody shells. Doesn't look like you needed my help, anyways."

"I was lucky," Manning stated. "Do me a favor and call the police. Have them gather up this trash. I've got a business appointment to keep, but I'll be happy to testify against these scum when I get back."

"But what should I do if they ask what your name is?" the old man inquired as he watched Manning head for his truck.

"Tell them the truth," the Phoenix Force powerhouse replied, climbing behind the wheel. "Tell them you don't know."

4

Calvin James followed Rafael Encizo around the coral reef off the Florida coast. Although a veteran diver and formerly a member of a U.S. Navy Seal team, James realized that Encizo was the more experienced diver of the pair. He knew he still had a lot to learn, and Encizo was the best frogman and UDT expert James had ever met.

James had spent a great deal of his twenty-eight years trying to prove himself to others. A black man from the Southside of Chicago, Calvin James had been a fighter all his life. Fistfights with white bigots, knife fights with black punks and the frustrating struggle to overcome poverty had been among his early battles.

At the age of seventeen, James joined the Navy. He became a hospital corpsman with the elite Seals and saw combat in Vietnam. He was decorated for valor and honorably discharged to continue a career in medicine and chemistry with the help of the GI bill.

Then criminals struck down his mother and younger sister. Not unlike Mack Bolan, Calvin James went to war against crime. However, unlike the Executioner, James tried to work within the system. He became a police officer and eventually earned a position with the San Francisco SWAT team. Yet James remained a maverick by nature and never really fit in anywhere until Stony Man recruited him for Phoenix Force.

A medic, frogman, chemist, an expert with small arms and a second *dan* black belt in *tae kwon do*, Calvin James was a perfect choice for the unique antiterrorist team. He did not feel he had to prove himself to the other members of Phoenix Force. That had already been achieved during his first mission with the team. But James knew he had to improve his skills and acquire new abilities. Phoenix Force consisted of the very best. And the best never stop trying to get better.

RAFAEL ENCIZO PADDLED his finned feet gently as he swam toward the sandy bottom of the cove. The ocean was filled with life. Polyp flowers jutted from the mud. A variety of brightly colored small fish darted among the sea grass, and an occasional crab cowered into the vegetation to hide from the strange beings in rubber wet suits who had invaded the underwater world.

The Cuban knew this world well, and he appreciated the fact that man was always an outsider. He thought the ocean was like a woman—beautiful, fascinating and dangerous. A man's survival underwater depended on his keeping his head at all times and following the strict rules that anyone who ventured into the deep must obey. Failure could mean a painful death.

Encizo was no stranger to danger. He accepted danger as a natural part of life. Thirteen years older than Calvin James, Encizo's background was even more violent. Virtually his entire family had been slaughtered by the Communists in Cuba. Encizo had fought Castro's brutal minions until he was forced to flee to the United States.

He was among the freedom fighters who landed on the Cuban shores during the Bay of Pigs Invasion in 1961. Captured by the Communists and held prisoner in El Principe, Castro's infamous political prison, Encizo suffered through days of starvation and torture. But the jailers could not break Rafael Encizo. Instead, he broke a sentry's neck and escaped.

Encizo returned to the United States, became a naturalized citizen and eventually found employment as an insurance investigator specializing in maritime claims. Before that, the Cuban worked at a variety of jobs, from treasure hunter to scuba instructor and professional bodyguard. Yet he never lost his desire to fight the enemies of freedom and individuality.

Rafael Encizo was an ideal recruit for Phoenix Force. A veteran of a thousand battles, he was absolutely fearless in combat. He was fanatically loyal to friends and totally ruthless to his enemies.

THE MEN WERE EQUIPPED with Emerson closed-circuit breathing apparatuses. The Emerson had been standard equipment for the United States Navy since 1963, and both Encizo and James were familar with the unit. Although it had a dry-land weight of thirty-five pounds, the Emerson was surprisingly buoyant underwater. Encizo liked the fact that it was equipped with a maximum self-contained-cylinder oxygen supply of one hundred sixty minutes, though he usually kept training exercises to dives no longer than ninety minutes.

For Encizo, it was a temptation to stay underwater. The ocean was a thrilling, fascinating realm, unlike anything on the land. Sunlight sparkled like floating diamonds overhead. Colors seemed different, brighter and magnified by the water. Fish and other sea life were constantly moving.

A diver could never be sure what creatures of the deep he might encounter or how they would react to his presence. Most darted away in fear. Others were curious and swam boldly forward to investigate the strange new visitor to their universe.

And some considered man to be just another potential meal.

Encizo saw the first shark in the distance. A six-foot-long gray torpedo, it glided gracefully through the water. Its unmistakable dorsal fin resembled the blade of a knife, as it swam with the swift ease of a predator at home in its stalking ground.

The Cuban looked at Calvin James. The black man nodded to confirm that he had also seen the shark. Encizo saw James's eyes through the lens of his face mask. James's expression seemed calm. Good, the Cuban thought, Calvin is keeping his head. Good man.

Anyone who spent much time in the ocean eventually encountered sharks. Experienced divers like James and Encizo learned to take the presence of the great predator fish in stride. Sharks seldom attacked people. There were more than two hundred species of shark, but only nine were known to be man-eaters.

The tiger shark, however, belonged to that minority.

Two more tiger sharks appeared. They glided to the first fish, and Encizo and James watched the deadly trio swim in formation, stalking the water for prey. Encizo knew that the killer fish relied on their keen sense of smell. A shark could detect blood half a mile away. This triggered a biochemical that sent a command to the animal's primitive brain to attack. This order was obligatory. The shark *had to* attack.

A small octopus sensed danger and floated to the floor of the cove. It crawled to the polyp bed and flattened itself along the surface. The little cephalopod activated its chromatophore cells, which allowed it to change color and blend with the sand.

Encizo and James could not camouflage themselves at will. They used the next best tactic—they remained perfectly still. Sharks were attracted by movement, and with a little luck the fish would move on to more promising territory and leave the divers to continue their exercise.

Suddenly a great gray blur shot out from the reef. The monstrous form brushed against Encizo. The Cuban was spun about by the blow and knocked into the coral. Encizo's arm raked the rough surface.

The fabric of his wet suit tore open, and Encizo fought to control his breath—holding one's breath or gulping canister gas increased the risk of carbon dioxide poisoning.

Blood oozed from Encizo's scraped arm, forming a dark cloud in the water. The effect the scent had on the sharks was inescapable.

The giant beast that had struck Encizo turned swiftly and headed toward the wounded Cuban. The tiger shark was almost nine feet long and probably weighed close to eight hundred pounds. Yet it rocketed through the water like a bullet. Its jaws hung open, revealing a mouthful of razor-sharp triangular teeth.

Rafael Encizo was fast, but no man was as quick as a shark in water. Still, the Cuban moved in time to avoid the deadly lunge. The shark's powerful jaws struck the reef, and coral chipped off from the tremendous impact. The shark kept moving. It turned around in a rapid, smooth circle and charged again.

So far the other sharks had not joined the giant. The attacking shark ignored Calvin James, guided by the scent of blood from the Cuban's scraped arm. But James did not intend simply to watch his friend become fish food. The black man drew his USMC knife from the sheath strapped to his ankle and launched himself at the shark.

As James collided with the great fish he felt as if he had tried to tackle a speeding freight train. The commando struck out with his knife even as the force of the hurtling shark knocked him backward. The mouthpiece of the Emerson regulator slipped from his teeth when he rolled away from the man-eater.

The warrior replaced his mouthpiece and carefully inhaled. He gazed up at the shark. The fish thrashed about violently, while James's knife jutted from the side of the shark's head. James had stabbed the blade under the operculum and thrust it into a gill.

Enraged with pain, the killer fish whirled and dived for Calvin James. Encizo had time to draw his Gerber Mark II diver's knife. He moved under the shark and plunged upward to drive the blade into the belly of the great fish.

The shark's own momentum contributed to the damage caused by the knife blade. Sharp steel slit a long gash in the trunk of the monster. Blood and entrails spilled from the terrible wound. A thick column of dark fog soon surrounded the injured shark.

The torrent of blood immediately attracted the other sharks that had been circling the area, uncertain whether to stay or move on. They no longer hesitated. The three predators rushed forward and attacked the wounded fish. None of them had further interest in the two men. Even the injured tiger shark was caught up in the blood-lust frenzy, snapping up and swallowing its own entrails while the other fish continued to tear it apart.

JAMES AND ENCIZO SURFACED and climbed onto the ladder of the *Diana*, a small trawler that belonged to José López. The Hispanic captain helped the divers into the boat, where they removed their face masks and the mouthpieces of their regulators. Both men sighed with relief and breathed fresh air greedily, happy to still be alive.

"Man," Calvin James muttered. "Your training exercises are a real bitch, Rafael."

"Rafael," López began as he helped Encizo unstrap his Emerson tank, "there was an urgent message for you on the radio while you were diving with Senor James."

"'Urgent'?" the Cuban asked, unbuckling his weight belt.

"*Sí,*" López replied. "Somebody in Washington is trying to get in touch with you."

"Oh, that." Encizo shrugged, concealing the importance of the message from López. "I know what it's about. Let's turn this boat around and head for shore, José. Buy you a beer, amigo."

"You got a deal, Rafael." López smiled. "Probably a good idea to leave now. I think I saw a shark a couple minutes ago."

"No shit?" James remarked dryly.

5

Manning, Encizo and James met Yakov Katzenelenbogen in the conference room of a Holiday Inn at the
outskirts of Frederick, Maryland. The Israeli had
told his teammates about the Bulgarians and terrorists assembled on Krio Island.

"This is the man with the money," Katz began as
he handed a photograph to Gary Manning. "Dimitri
Krio."

"I've heard a lot about Krio," the Canadian remarked. "But I don't recall ever seeing a picture of
him before."

"Is it a recent photo?" Rafael Encizo inquired. "I
thought Krio hadn't appeared in public for almost
ten years now."

"Eight and a half," Katz supplied. "Give or take a
month. The photo was taken last week."

"I hate to sound ignorant," Calvin James inter-
jected, "but I never heard of this Krio dude before
today."

"Not many people are familiar with the name,"
Katz told him.

"The rest of you guys seem to know about him."
The black man shrugged. "Or did you set this up to
make me look dumb?"

"Gary and I have been involved with international

trade," the Israeli explained. "Rafael probably remembers the name from his days as a maritime investigator."

"Dimitri Krio is a Greek shipping tycoon," Encizo stated. "He's probably worth about a quarter of a billion dollars."

"Oh, yeah?" James raised his eyebrows. "I gotta see this guy."

Encizo handed the photo to the black commando. Dimitri Krio's round face was deeply tanned. His thick mane of silver hair was carefully styled and combed. Lines at the corners of his mouth suggested Krio smiled a lot. Why not, James thought. If I had a quarter of a billion dollars, I'd be smiling, too.

But James did not like Krio's smile. Somehow the twin rows of perfectly capped white teeth reminded him of the open jaws of the tiger shark.

"A quarter of a billion, huh?" James shrugged. "I wouldn't pay that much for him."

"Nonetheless," Katz said as he flicked the ash from a cigarette into an ashtray, "Krio has earned more since he inherited his father's shipping company in 1957. It's difficult to estimate how wealthy the man really is. He has at least one Swiss bank account the Greek tax collectors don't know about, and it's believed he's involved with a number of secret ventures that also net a large profit Krio doesn't report for obvious reasons."

"Like dealing with the Bulgarian secret police." James frowned. "Why would a wealthy Western capitalist do business with the Communists?"

"It happens all the time," Manning stated. "Armand Hammer, Cyrus Eaton, David Rockefeller and a lot of other American millionaires have done plenty of business with the Soviet Union. Moscow never fails to give them the VIP treatment. So much for the Communist sermon about how much they despise the nasty capitalist rich.''

"Dimitri Krio isn't exactly Aristotle Onassis," Encizo added. "Onassis earned his fortune. He worked for it from the beginning. Krio inherited much of his. Onassis was never fond of dealing with Marxist countries, but Krio seems to specialize in it. His shipping lines extend to Syria, Libya and Angola. Krio does a lot of import-export trade with the Eastern European countries. Especially Yugoslavia and Bulgaria.''

"But from what Yakov told us Krio has a bunch of international terrorists as houseguests on his island," James declared. "That seems kinda hard to believe.''

"But it isn't unprecedented," Katz told him. "The late Giangiacomo Feltrinelli frequently had such infamous terrorists as Ulrike Meinhof and Augusto Viel as houseguests. Feltrinelli was an Italian publisher, very wealthy and successful and an absolute political fanatic. He helped finance a number of terrorist organizations throughout Western Europe.''

"Do you think that's what Krio is doing in Greece?" Manning inquired.

"That's what we have to find out," Katz answered. "What makes this situation especially critical is the fact that Kostov and Vitosho are among Krio's guests. You all realize that the Bulgarian government is virtually an extension of the Kremlin. Thus, the Bulgarian secret police is actually a branch of the Russian KGB.''

"Yeah," Encizo said grimly. "And lately it appears the KGB is using the Bulgarians to handle operations that are too hot for Moscow to want to be directly connected with."

"Exactly," Katz agreed. "That's why we have to find out what's happening on Krio Island."

"This sounds like a recon mission," James said as he frowned. "I thought Phoenix Force was designed to seek and destroy. Isn't gathering intelligence a job for the CIA and the rest of those sneaky-pete dudes?"

"Regular intel sources haven't been very successful so far," the Israeli replied. "Before we can seek and destroy we have to make sure we have the right targets."

"I'm sure." Encizo shrugged. "The island is crawling with enemy agents and terrorists. What more proof do we need?"

"We can't just fly to Greece and blast Krio Island to hell," Katz told him. "Krio is a wealthy, influential man. If we launch a raid on his property, we'd better be able to prove we had just cause. Otherwise we run the risk of stirring up an international incident that might be more valuable to the KGB for propaganda purposes than whatever Krio is up to on his island."

"How do you want to handle this, Yakov?" Manning asked.

"Krio has been trying to get shipping operations here in the Western Hemisphere," the colonel began. "So far he hasn't had much luck. He'd probably be happy to see a couple of representatives from an American import-export corporation who are interested in doing business with him."

"Sounds like I'm getting a chance to volunteer," Encizo said dryly.

"You know the shipping business," Katz stated. "And you're the only member of the team who understands Greek."

"I only know a few hundred words in Greek," the Cuban replied. "I'm not even sure I can put together a proper sentence in the language anymore."

"Brush up on it for the next day or so," Katz advised. "You're going to be the West Coast manager of Exotic Imports Unlimited. Now your traveling companion will be the East Coast distributor."

"Don't look at me," James said. "I've never been a businessman. I'm just an ex-cop you guys conned into joining this nutty outfit."

"Sounds like I'm volunteer number two," Manning stated. "So we've got a day or two to get ready?"

"You and Rafael have," the Israeli confirmed. "Calvin and I will leave tonight. Brognola can arrange a military flight to Greece, and we'll be able to transport whatever weapons and equipment we might need for the mission. You two will fly out on a commercial airliner to avoid suspicion."

"We won't be able to take much gear with us." Encizo frowned. "Not if we're going to get through airport security without a hassle."

"That'll depend on how clever you are." Katz grinned.

"What about David?" Encizo asked, referring to the fifth member of Phoenix Force.

"McCarter will meet us in Greece," Katz replied. "He ought to be on his way there by now."

DAVID MCCARTER LIT another cigarette as he sat in the plastic scoop-backed chair in the lobby leading to gate twenty-two. He glanced at the luminous hands of his black-faced Le Gran wristwatch and clucked his tongue in disgust. Twenty minutes remained before the bloody plane would be ready to board.

The tall, fox-faced Briton hated to travel by commercial airline. An ace pilot who could fly anything from a hot-air balloon to a 747, McCarter would have preferred to fly himself to Greece. His second choice was a military flight. However, Major Hillerman had not been able to arrange that luxury on this occasion.

The major was a good sort in McCarter's opinion, and he had never been one to care much for officers. Hillerman had been McCarter's SAS commanding officer during the Omani Ohofar War back in the seventies. The Special Air Service regiment operated in Oman for five years. Twelve SAS men were killed during that campaign, but Hillerman and McCarter "beat the clock," as people liked to say at SAS headquarters in Hereford.

So far both men had continued to "beat the clock." Hillerman lost his leg in Oman, but he gained a promotion to field-grade officer and was later transferred to Special Military Intelligence. McCarter remained in the SAS and participated in Operation Nimrod. To be part of the successful SAS siege of the Iranian embassy in London and the rescue of twenty hostages from the terrorists who had seized the building was the high point of McCarter's career.

Then the Briton was chosen for the Phoenix Force team. The five-man commando army had since suc-

cessfully accomplished more than a dozen missions.
To David McCarter that was just fine. He felt that a
man was never more alive than in combat. Anger,
fear, excitement and the pure joy of adrenaline
coursing through the veins like a narcotic all reached
their peak in combat.

McCarter was not simply a thrill junkie or a war
lover. He believed in fighting the enemies of England
and the rest of the free world. He would never do
anything contrary to the best interests of his nation.
Yet he was the first to admit that the battlefield was
his favorite element.

Hillerman was unaware of McCarter's connection
with Phoenix Force. The major knew McCarter was
involved in some sort of top-secret business that had
the blessing of MI6, SIS, the PM and other important sources that favor initials. Hillerman had been
ordered to cooperate with McCarter and see to his
former sergeant's needs.

McCarter and Hillerman got along well together.
Many people found McCarter's short temper and
sharp tongue difficult to tolerate. His wry sense of
humor, dedication to duty and exceptional courage
compensated for his flaws. McCarter almost smiled
as he recalled one of Hillerman's comments: "In
order to appreciate McCarter, you've got to be in
combat with the bugger."

Although Hillerman had failed to get a military
flight for McCarter, he had arranged to transport the
combat veteran's weapons and equipment. His gear
would be waiting for him with a case officer at the
British Embassy, Ploutarkhou Street in Athens.

McCarter was in a surly mood. He did not like

working a mission without knowing the details. He did not like being unarmed. And he damn well did not like sitting on his arse in a London airport, waiting for a bloody civilian plane to get ready to finally get off the ground.

A swarthy man dressed in a tweed suit two sizes too large for his wiry frame entered the lobby. McCarter noticed that the man's right hand was jammed inside his coat pocket. The bulge suggested his fist was clenched. The Phoenix Force commando stiffened as the stranger approached.

"You are Mr. McCarter?" he asked, his accent revealing English was not his native language.

"I'm waiting for a plane, mate," McCarter replied. He rapidly tried to think of the best way to handle the situation, considering the abundance of innocent bystanders in the lobby.

"You will come with me," the stranger demanded. "I have a hand grenade in my pocket. The pin has already been removed. If I release the spoon, the grenade will explode in three seconds. I do not wish to kill all these people, but if I must. . . ."

"I know," the Briton muttered. "I've met lunatics like you before. I'm coming. All right?"

McCarter rose from his chair and allowed the stranger to escort him through the hallway. The Briton considered the possibility that the swarthy man was bluffing about the grenade. He probably was lying, or he would have simply used it in the lobby. Terrorists do not care about killing innocent victims.

But McCarter cared, and he could not take that risk. Meantime, the stranger had not killed him, and as long as the Briton was alive, there was a chance he might be able to turn the tables on his captor.

"What outfit are you with, chum?" McCarter asked as the stranger led him to the gentlemen's room. "Black September? Palestine Protection Front? Arab People's Liberation Army?"

"Iranian Patriotic League," the terrorist replied bluntly.

"Never heard of that one," McCarter remarked. "You chaps specialize in killing blokes in the loo because it's a place you can relate to?"

"Get in the bathroom, English!" the Iranian growled.

McCarter noticed an Out of Order sign on the door as he pushed it open. He was not surprised when the terrorist shoved him into the room. McCarter did not try to resist. He purposely staggered forward into the closest sink. The Briton pretended to be dazed as he turned to face his opponent.

"No grenade, English," the Iranian announced with a grin. He drew a diminutive .25-caliber Bauer automatic from his pocket. "Only this."

"Well, that's enough," McCarter gasped, clutching his rib cage. "What's all this about?"

"You hurt yourself on the sink, English?" the terrorist chuckled. "I thought SAS were supposed to be tough."

"This bloody sink isn't made of foam rubber, damn it," McCarter gritted through clenched teeth. "Why do you want to kill me?"

"You killed my brothers at the embassy," the Iranian declared. "We're going to avenge them. All you SAS scum will pay with your lives for your slaughter of our patriots."

"I was just following orders," the Briton insisted. He gestured helplessly with his left hand, while the right still clutched his ribs. "You would have done the same if...."

"Begging for mercy, infidel?" the Iranian grinned.

"I'm not an infidel," McCarter replied. "And you're not acting by the word of the Koran. Doesn't the book begin with the passage, 'In the name of Allah, the merciful and compassionate'? But you show neither mercy nor compassion."

"You're a Muslim?" the terrorist asked with surprise and suspicion. He automatically stepped closer.

"When I was in Oman," McCarter began, leaning toward his captor. "Years ago, I met a very wise man. He spoke about the Koran and the Prophet...."

"He was probably a Sunni Muslim," the Iranian scoffed. "The Sunni are our enemies, the same as the Jews and the Christians."

"Your enemies aren't based on the Koran," the Briton declared as he stepped closer. "Allah sent down the Torah and the Gospel as guidance to the people, and He sent salvation...."

McCarter's right arm suddenly lashed a fast sideways stroke as he turned his entire body away from the gun. The little Bauer uttered a crisp crack, and its .25-caliber projectile ricocheted against a tile wall.

The Briton grabbed his opponent's wrist with his right hand and jammed his left elbow into the man's armpit. McCarter locked the man's arm in a painful hold and yanked hard. The gun fell from the terrorist's fingers.

The Iranian punted a foot into the back of McCarter's knee and the Briton's leg buckled. In sudden and severe pain McCarter fell to one knee, but he held on to the terrorist's arm and pulled. The assassin cried out as he hurled over the Englishman's bowed head.

McCarter leaped to his feet. His left leg was numb from the Iranian's kick, but no bones were broken or muscles cramped. The terrorist rolled across the floor and reached for a dagger in an ankle sheath. McCarter lunged forward and slammed a karate side kick into the man's chest.

The Iranian fell against a urinal. He lashed a kick at McCarter. The Briton dodged the foot, but the terrorist had ample time to rise from the floor. The Iranian did not try to draw the knife. He assumed a T-*dachi* stance, hands held ready, fingers rigid like a pair of fighting blades.

McCarter quickly adopted a Wing-Chuan position. His open hands poised to defend the "four gates" to his torso's vulnerable spots. The Iranian swung a foot at McCarter's groin. The Briton's foot rapped into his shin before the kick could connect. The terrorist stabbed a fingertip thrust for McCarter's throat. The commando parried the spear-hand attack with his right hand and jabbed a left fist to the point of his opponent's jaw.

The terrorist's head snapped back from the impact of the punch. McCarter swiftly slashed the side of his right hand across the Iranian's exposed throat. Blood splurted from the man's open mouth as he clamped both hands to his crushed windpipe and crumbled to the floor.

"Thanks for the salvation," McCarter said breathlessly.

The Briton used a handkerchief to gather up the little .25 automatic. Then he checked the Iranian's pulse to be certain the man was dead. He was. McCarter felt grateful no one had ignored the Out of Order sign on the door. He did not want to waste time explaining a fresh corpse to airport security.

He dragged the Iranian into one of the stalls and sat the corpse on the toilet. McCarter used the handkerchief to avoid leaving prints on the gun as he pressed the magazine catch. The ammo clip dropped into the dead man's lap.

McCarter did not intend to leave a loaded gun lying about. Some damn fool might find it and cause an accident. He worked the slide to pop a round out of the chamber, wiped off the Bauer once more and dropped it into a trash barrel.

The British ace calmly emerged from the washroom and lit another cigarette. Fortunately the report of the little .25 auto had not attracted anyone's attention. McCarter was thankful his opponent had not chosen a larger caliber weapon.

He returned to gate twenty-two in time to hear the announcement that the flight to Athens, Greece, was ready to receive passengers.

6

Colonel Nicolai Kostov liked Greece. The climate was more agreeable than in his native Bulgaria. The people were generally pleasant, the food was good and the standard of living was better than average—if one looked at it on an international level.

Yet Kostov also remembered a different Greece. He recalled the occupation by German and Italian soldiers during World War II. Bulgaria had been an ally of the Nazis at the beginning of the war, but in 1944, Bulgaria had turned against the Axis powers to support the Soviet Union.

Kostov had been a young man then, but already involved in the world of espionage. He was part of a team of Bulgarian communists that slipped into Greece to assist members of the Communist resistance movement known as the Kokino Lionta'ris.

The "Red Lions" conducted a series of hit-and-run attacks against the Germans. One night the young Kostov personally took out a Nazi staff car with a Molotov cocktail. Two men burst from the fiery automobile, their bodies shrouded in flame. Kostov heard them scream and smelled the sickeningly sweet stench of burning human flesh. The young Bulgarian fell to his knees. Both arms hugged his heaving stomach as he opened his mouth and vomited on the grass. A Greek partisan ended the suffering of the flaming Nazis with a volley of 9mm rounds from a confiscated Schmeisser MP-40 submachine gun. Kostov was unaware an enemy soldier was aiming a gun at his back. He would have been killed if another Greek had not seized the German from behind and plunged a knife between his ribs.

"Ineh indaski, Nicolai," a veteran commando assured Kostov as he helped the lad to his feet. "It is all right, Nicolai. You have done well, boy."

After the war, Bulgaria became a satellite of the USSR. Kostov was once again sent to Greece to assist the Communists in an unsuccessful revolution against the Greek monarchist government. The Kokino Lionta'ris were reunited, but the Greeks branded them as bandits instead of heroes. In 1949, the civil war ended and Kostov returned to Bulgaria. He was the only survivor of the Red Lion commandos left.

The Soviet Union, which owned Bulgaria lock, stock and puppet government, recognized Kostov's potential. The KGB recruited the Bulgarian intelligence officer to serve with Department Eleven, the Eastern European Control Section.

Kostov was a highly motivated operative. He tended to regard all non-Communists as simply different versions of the old Nazi regime. Kostov felt a worldwide Communist government was the only hope of crushing the Hitlerian powers he believed to exist.

Years of experience and assignments in various countries had altered Kostov's former zeal. He realized most of the Soviet Union's propaganda was false. He knew the KGB specialized in subversion and terrorism. Kostov had been able to compare Communist societies with the democracies of West Germany, Italy and Greece. He saw for himself that the latter offered its citizens more rights, freedom and a higher standard of living than the former.

However, Nicolai Kostov had become part of the sinister bureaucracy of the Russian KGB. His dedication to the Party had earned him the godlike prestige and power of a field-grade officer in Department Eleven. Power is addictive. Kostov was not about to jeopardize his position of authority.

That didn't mean he had to like this newest assignment that had brought him back to Greece. Yet he would carry out the mission with his usual professional determination and skill. He was too proud to lower the standards of his work and too old to start disobeying orders from the Kremlin.

THE BULGARIAN COLONEL sat in a deck chair on the marble patio with Dimitri Krio. The sun bathed Kostov with pleasant heat as he gazed out at the beautiful Mediterranean Sea that surrounded the island. A servant brought the pair a tray of *dolmatehs* and a bottle of Inos Lefkos, vintage 1967.

"*Efkahri stoh, Milo,*" Krio told his servant. "That will be all for now."

Milo nodded and headed for the door.

Kostov noticed a slight bulge in the white jacket under the servant's left arm. The Bulgarian turned to his host. "His jacket is too tight to properly conceal a shoulder holster rig," Kostov remarked. "If you insist that he be armed, I suggest you have him carry his weapon in a holster at the small of his back."

"I will remember your advice, Tungirio Kostov." Krio smiled. "Eat. I'm sure you'll find the *dolmatehs* to your liking."

"I've no doubt of that, comrade," the Bulgarian agreed. "But there are other matters that are less than satisfactory."

"You worry too much, my friend," Krio insisted as he adjusted his gold-frame aviator glasses. "The authorities have taken an interest in us? They spy on me from time to time. The Greek government doesn't like the fact I do business with the Communists, so I must endure such petty harassment. Yet they can do nothing about my choice of business associates. That is free enterprise, eh?"

Krio laughed, but Kostov was not amused. "They are suspicious," the Bulgarian declared.

"They have no grounds to support their suspicions." Krio shrugged. "I am not a Communist. Everyone knows I'm a member of the panhellenic socialist movement. I have friends in parliament who will vouch for my patriotism to the Republic of Greece."

"Do you think they'll support you if they learn you're harboring a small army of international terrorists on this island?"

" 'Terrorists'?" Krio raised his eyebrows. "Do you not mean the noble warriors of the great revolution against the oppressive bourgeoisie?"

"Call them what you wish," Kostov said bluntly. "Gerhart, Khatid and several of the others are wanted men. You cannot expect to keep a low profile when you have known murderers, kidnappers and saboteurs on this island."

"Your comrades in the KGB sent them to me," the Greek remarked. "Moscow is 'calling the shots,' as the Americans might say."

"Moscow makes mistakes," Kostov stated. "And I'm beginning to think this mission is one of them."

"Are you still concerned about that Greek intelligence agent?" Krio sighed as he poured himself a glass of wine. "The spy did not learn a thing while he was here."

"The man was on this island for two days. . . ."

"But we knew about him even before he arrived," Krio insisted. "Thanks to my own intelligence sources in Athens. It was easy to keep him ignorant until he left."

"He will still be able to supply information," Kostov declared. "He can give details about the island and the house."

"The authorities have surely made maps of the island and copied the blueprints of this house long ago," Krio remarked. "The spy will have little to add to what they already know. However, whatever assistance he may have been to them, he will not be in any condition to supply further information now."

"What does that mean?" the Bulgarian demanded. "Don't tell me you gave him a dose of the Proteus Enzyme," Kostov said accusingly.

"Consider it another field experiment, comrade." Krio laughed.

"You fool!" Kostov snapped. "There was no need for that."

"Retribution," the Greek stated simply. "I dislike those scum sticking their anteater noses into my affairs."

"That was stupid," Kostov said. "It will only increase their suspicions."

"They cannot prove anything," Krio told him. "You know that."

"I do not like this," Kostov insisted. "Our security has already been jeopardized, and now you have agreed to let two Americans come here for a business meeting."

"If I had refused to meet with them that would truly be suspicious." Krio smiled. "I have been trying to get a connection with an American shipping company for almost a decade. I may as well make a profit from the United States now, as it won't be a world power much longer."

"Those Americans might be with the CIA."

"They will only be here for a few hours." The Greek shrugged. "Do not be concerned, comrade. Even if the Americans are spies, they will learn nothing."

"I do not like your recklessness, Krio," Kostov told him. "I have been in this business for a long time, and I have not been a success by working with careless people."

"Come now." Krio sighed. "Soon the last of the tests will be completed. Then the enzyme and our outlaw comrades will be on their way to various locations throughout the world."

"That cannot happen soon enough to suit me," the Bulgarian admitted.

"Indeed." Krio smiled. "The KGB will certainly reward you handsomely for this. A promotion to general, or perhaps you will even become the head of the Bulgarian State Security Service."

"I am not interested in personal glory," Kostov stated, although he knew this was not entirely true. "Or financial gain."

"My gain will benefit the KGB," the Greek said. "We will all profit, Comrade Colonel. You and your superiors in one way, and I in another. The world is about to change. Within a year the powers of the Western world will crumble and fall."

"A great many innocent people will suffer," Kostov remarked grimly. "I can find no pleasure in that."

"But war between East and West is inescapable." Krio shrugged. "You have said so yourself."

"I know." The Bulgarian nodded. "And I suppose the Proteus Enzyme is a better solution than a nuclear war."

"Much better," Krio assured him. "Whoever the genius in the Soviet Union is who conjured up this scheme ought to be the new premier. Not a shot will be fired. No radioactive contamination will result. And there will be no way for the capitalists to blame us for what will happen. It will appear to be what the idiot Christians would call 'an act of God.' "

"Or the devil," Kostov replied with a sad shake of his head.

7

Yakov Katzenelenbogen and Calvin James arrived at the Athens airport shortly after noon. They climbed from the U.S. Navy C-130 and hauled out three oblong-shaped aluminum suitcases. Katz waved his steel hook at the pilot. The air jockey nodded in return. He did not know who his two mysterious passengers were, but he had delivered them to Athens. His job was done.

A slender man dressed in a light-blue suit approached the pair. The face beneath the brim of his straw hat was well tanned and featured a pencil-thin mustache and a black patch over his left eye. The Phoenix Force commandos noticed the butt of a pistol peeking from a cross-draw holster under the guy's jacket.

"Welcome to Greece, gentlemen," he announced, his English containing only a trace of an accent. "Are you with the British embassy?"

The odd question was a password, and Katz replied with the correct counterphrase. "No," the Israeli said. "But can you help us find our friend from England?"

"As a matter of fact, I can." The Greek smiled. "Please follow me."

The Phoenix Force pair followed the stranger

through an open gate that led to the luggage transportation section. Katz glanced up at a sign written in Greek above the entrance. Some of the letters looked the same as Russian Cyrillic, but Katz could not translate a single word. The multilingual Israeli was not used to being in a country where he could not understand the native language. He did not like it. He felt ignorant and dependent on others.

"My name is Manos Draco," the one-eyed Greek explained as he led the Phoenix Force vets through the baggage section. "I'm with the National Security Service. I believe you call my position a 'case officer' in the CIA. Correct?"

"I'm Solomon Goldblum, and this is Jim Johnson," Katz replied, using their cover names.

"Your British friend arrived this morning." Draco laughed. "He seemed rather upset to be told the details of his mission from contacts here in Greece."

"We sort of figured he'd meet us at the airport so we could tell him ourselves," James remarked.

"Where is our friend?" Katz inquired.

"Mr. Miller." Draco smiled. "That's what he's calling himself. He's picking up a crate that was delivered to the British Embassy."

"All right." The Israeli nodded. "How well have you been briefed on this mission, Mr. Draco?"

"I probably know as much about the Krio business as anyone who isn't on that island with him. I'll tell you the details on the way to our safehouse. That's what you CIA people call a temporary base of operations, yes?"

"Your English is very good," James commented. "You've even got the Company jargon down pat."

"We were told you'd need translators," Draco continued. "I'm afraid Mr. Kalvo is upset about this business. He's the CIA case officer who was in charge until the new orders put you gentlemen in command. He's been stationed here for years and speaks Greek fluently. You three have sort of stolen his thunder."

"We'll straighten things out with Kalvo," Katz assured him.

"Right now he's with Mr. Miller," Draco commented. "I imagine your British friend and he have exchanged words by now."

"Oh, yeah." James nodded, familiar with McCarter's sharp tongue. "I bet they have at that."

The trio left the airport and headed for the parking lot. Draco escorted the newcomers to a Volkswagen Rabbit. They loaded the luggage in the car and climbed into the VW.

"What can you add to our information about the Krio affair?" Katz asked Draco.

"Not much, I'm afraid," the Greek confessed. "We managed to slip an agent into Krio's house. He was disguised as a caterer and stayed almost twenty-four hours. Somehow Krio must have known. Panayotis Sioris, the agent, was never allowed to venture beyond the house."

"He must have learned something," James insisted.

"We already have a detailed map of the island thanks to aerial reconnaissance," Draco explained. "Sioris drew up some crude blueprints of what he saw of the house. He also noted that most of Krio's servants are hired on a temporary basis. The permanent personnel are very tight-lipped, but they're obviously bodyguards as well, and carry pistols at all times."

"What did he find out about the Bulgarians and the terrorists?" James asked.

"Very little," the Greek said, steering his Rabbit onto the Arch of Hadrian. "Sioris never saw Kostov, but he recognized Captain Vitosho leading a group of men dressed in fatigue uniforms in some physical-training exercises. They were working out on a parade field located between two barracks. Krio claimed these are members of a new security corporation he's putting together. Training bodyguards for rich men like himself. Sioris didn't manage to get a better look at the billets."

"We'd better talk to this Sioris," Katz said.

"He can't tell you anything," Draco answered.

"Maybe hypnosis will help," James suggested. "Sioris might not consciously remember anything of value, but under hypnosis we can open up his subconscious and try to find out about little details he might have overlooked."

"You don't understand," the Greek began. "Sioris has become gravely ill since his mission."

"Ill?" James asked. "How ill?"

"He's been hospitalized after complaining about severe stomach pains," Draco explained. "The doctors believe he's suffering from a strange gastral disease. Sioris is literally unable to digest food."

"Dying of malnutrition," Katz said in astonishment, recalling the bizarre death of Uri Yosefthal.

"That is correct," Draco confirmed. "The doctors are quite baffled by this."

"No wonder." Calvin James frowned. The medic and chemistry expert considered possible causes. "Have they said anything about surgery?"

"I'm not sure," Draco admitted. "Apparently they don't want to cut, because they have no idea what's wrong."

"What about intravenous feeding?" James asked.

"That doesn't seem to work, either," Draco said.

"It didn't help Uri," Katz remarked grimly.

"What do you mean by that, Mr. Goldblum?" Draco inquired.

"A possible pattern," the Israeli answered. "Can we see Sioris?"

"He's in no condition to be questioned," the Greek stated. "The poor man is dying. . . ."

"He won't have to answer any questions," Yakov said. "But I want to see him immediately."

"You have an idea about what happened to the dude?" James asked.

"Perhaps," the Phoenix Force commander replied. "Frankly, I rather hope I'm wrong."

Manos Draco drove to the Accident and Orthopedic Hospital on Kifissia Road. The Greek intel officer's identification gained him an audience with Dr. Kessel, the MD in charge of Sioris's treatment.

Draco spoke to the portly, dour doctor in Greek. Katz and James could not understand the conversation, but Kessel's grim expression warned them that the translation would not be pleasant.

"Sioris's condition is worse," Draco told them. "He's gone into a coma. The doctor does not think he will live to see the sun set."

"I still want to see Sioris," Katz insisted.

"Mr. Goldblum," the Greek began. "The man is dying. Can't he be allowed to do so in peace?"

"There isn't time for such niceties," Yakov declared. "Too many lives are at stake. I simply want to see if his condition is the same as that of Uri Yosefthal when he died."

"Very well," Draco agreed sadly. "If you insist."

"I do," the Israeli confirmed.

KOSTA CHRYSOSTOMOS SMILED as he watched Dr. Kessel through the Bushnell 8x30 binoculars. Kessel pulled the bed sheet over the face of Panayotis Sioris, who lay in a hospital bed in a room across the street from Chrysostomos's hotel room. The invalid was dead. Chrysostomos and his partner, Constantine Mercouri, had been cooped up in that hotel for the past five days, waiting for Sioris to die.

Twenty-four-hour surveillance of a dying man seemed absurd to Chrysostomos, but he was paid well to obey orders and not ask too many questions. His employers rewarded loyalty and punished disobedience swiftly and ruthlessly.

Chrysostomos and Mercouri were Greek gangsters. They had started their violent careers as members of the infamous Lima'ni Fi'dis. The "Harbor Snakes" was a vicious gang that prowled the dockyards of Piraeus and Vouliagment. A pack of young savages, the Snakes preyed on careless drunks and lone fishermen. Now and then they assaulted young lovers who were drawn to the romantic shoreline without considering the possible hazard of strolling the piers after dark.

Eventually the hoodlums graduated beyond adolescent crime to find employment as enforcers for a loan-shark organization. Chrysostomos and Mercouri were sent to punish their employer's clients who failed to pay their loans promptly. Breaking arms and legs and disfiguring faces led to an occasional contract killing.

One night the hoodlums discovered their employer sprawled across his desk. His throat had been sliced open. Blood soaked into the ink blotter. Two men waited for the thugs. Both held Czech machine pistols.

The gunmen told them a new leader was now in charge of the loan-shark business. They could either work for the new boss or they would be splattered all over the walls of the office. Naturally Mercouri and Chrysostomos chose the former.

They had worked for their new employer for almost two years. Neither man realized that Dimitri Krio was the man in control. The shipping tycoon paid better than the deceased mobster kingpin and the men were generally given simple assignments that involved little risk. If a thug got arrested for assault, Krio arranged for a good lawyer and often bribed the judge to reduce the sentence. If Greece got too hot for one of his button men, Krio had him smuggled out of the country until things cooled off. His shipping trade made this quite easy.

The hoods believed they were part of a new criminal syndicate in Greece. This was only part of Krio's plan. He was actually creating his own personal intelligence network, with the unsuspecting gangsters as his agents.

Chrysostomos did not know why they had been

ordered to keep watch on the man in the hospital bed. He assumed the invalid was a member of a rival syndicate, or perhaps a troublesome police investigator. The reason did not matter. The job had been tiresome and boring.

Chrysostomos saw another figure approach the lifeless form lying on the hospital bed. The Greek hoodlum trained his binoculars on the man who pulled the sheet away from Sioris's face. The stranger had a metal device with three steel hooks instead of a right hand. A tall black man soon appeared beside the foreigner with the steel "hand."

"Constantine!" Chrysostomos snapped. "Come here!"

"What is wrong, Kosta?" Mercouri asked as he hurried to the window.

"The two men who arrived on the American military airplane are visiting the sick one in the hospital," Chrysostomos explained, handing the field glasses to his partner.

"Are you certain of this?" Mercouri frowned.

"See for yourself," Chrysostomos told him. "A Negro and a man with one hand. That is the description we received from Xerxes. Right?"

"Right," Mercouri agreed when he examined the hospital room through the Bushnell spyglass. "You are right, but the sick one is dead. We need only report the fact that the Americans have come here. Then we can go home."

"Don't be a fool," Chrysostomos snapped. "Those two must be important. Why else would we have been told to watch for them. I'm going to contact Xerxes right now."

"Do you think he will order us to follow these Americans?" Mercouri asked wearily.

"Probably," Chrysostomos answered. "Unless he wants us to kill them immediately."

8

"I wondered when the hell you blokes would finally get here," David McCarter told Katz and James when the three Phoenix Force members met in the safehouse on Ditamou Street.

"Glad to see you, too," Katz said dryly.

The trio had assembled in the Spartan kitchen, where McCarter had just pried open a wooden crate. He removed an aluminum case similar to the luggage Katz and James had brought with them on the C-130.

We arrived about three hours ago," the Israeli explained. "We're late because we stopped by the hospital to see Sioris."

"Kalvo told me about him." The Briton nodded. "How's he doing?"

"He's dead," Calvin James replied.

"Sounds like a permanent condition," the Briton remarked. "I heard the poor bastard wasn't able to digest food."

"That's right," the black commando replied. "I assisted with the autopsy. I've never seen anything like it before. Dude's stomach was full of moldy, rotten food. Stuff didn't digest, but it still decayed. Must have caused five different types of food poisoning."

"They should have pumped his stomach and fed

him intravenously,'' McCarter said as he worked the combination lock to his metal case.

"That wouldn't have saved him,'' James replied. "Sioris's pancreatic and intestinal fluids didn't work. The peritoneum was ruined. The pylorus, gastric glands and large and small intestines all failed to function. Liver, mesenteric artery were both useless. Even the serum in the blood wouldn't retain nutriments.''

"What could have caused that to happen?'' McCarter asked.

"I don't have any idea,'' James admitted. "Yakov has the only answer that might make sense.''

"Well, don't keep me in suspense, Katz,'' McCarter said as he opened his case and smiled. It contained a Browning Hi-Power autoloading pistol and a compact M-10 Ingram machine pistol. Both weapons were in 9mm parabellum caliber. They were also David McCarter's favorite tools of the trade. In addition, the case contained spare magazines for both firearms, as well as a Bianchi shoulder holster rig for the Browning and three SAS "bang-flash" concussion grenades.

McCarter's mood improved as he handled his weapons. Katz explained about Uri Yosefthal's death while the SAS warrior slid into his shoulder rig and nestled the pistol into leather under his left arm.

"The bloody KGB must be responsible for this,'' McCarter declared.

"That's what we figure,'' James agreed. "The bastards must have tested some sort of new chemical or biological weapon on Yosefthal. Probably used it on other political prisoners in their labor camps, as well.''

"The Soviets released Yosefthal because they knew he was going to die," Katz stated. "And no one would be able to prove the KGB was responsible, since the effects of their murderous chemistry didn't materialize until Yosefthal was transplanted to the United States."

"And now the Bulgarians have the chemical," James added. "No surprise about that, since the Bulgarian secret police are controlled by the KGB."

"That must mean the Communists and Krio are working on the starvation chemical on the island," McCarter stated.

"Seems to me they've already perfected it," James commented. "But they might be making more of the compound there."

"I've seen aerial photographs of the island," the Englishman told his partners. "There are several large buildings there. Any one of them could contain a chemistry laboratory."

"But why would they produce it on Krio Island?" James wondered aloud. "They could do it with greater security within the Soviet Union."

"There are two possible reasons," Katz began. "You're the chemist, Cal. What's the greatest danger involved in chemical-biological warfare?"

"Controlling a viruslike strain," James answered. "I see your point, Yakov. The KGB might have insisted that the chemicals be produced outside the iron curtain because they were afraid of a possible epidemic."

"Or they may intend to use the terrorists as agents to transfer the chemical to cities throughout the world for sabotage purposes," Katz added.

"Of course," McCarter agreed with the latter theory. "Krio doesn't have a terrorist training camp in the usual sense. It's a base for using terrorists as agents for chemical-biological warfare sabotage. From what Draco and Kalvo have told me about Krio, such a scheme fits his style."

"Kalvo is the CIA guy, right?" James asked. "Draco warned us that he doesn't like us horning in on his turf."

"Bloody right he doesn't," McCarter confirmed. "Expect some flak from that one. Kalvo was really pissed-off when we had to go to the British Embassy to get my crate. Thinks I'm with Her Majesty's Secret Service, or something like that. He doesn't see why he should take orders from us. Can't blame him for being upset, since he's been in Greece for a long time and speaks the language like a native. Probably is annoying to have a bunch of outsiders arrive and take over command."

"Where is Kalvo now?" Katz inquired.

"Filing a complaint about this situation to his control officer at the American embassy," McCarter said.

"That won't change anything." The Israeli shrugged. "Our authority comes from the Oval Office, so Kalvo can just grit his teeth and follow orders. Now what were you saying about Krio's style?"

"Oh, converting thugs to work in an intelligence network is sort of a Krio speciality," the Briton explained. "The coppers believe Krio is actually the power behind the second largest criminal syndicate in Greece. Clever bastard appears to have set up a sort of private spy ring, using hoodlums for field operations—recon, general intel and assassination."

"Oh, shit," James muttered. "There are supposed to be about a hundred guys on the island alone, and now you tell us we have to worry about a bunch of Krio's hired goons here as well?"

"Hell." McCarter shrugged. "Why worry about it? We've figured out what Krio is up to. Let's tell Draco and Kalvo. Then we'll see about getting a strike force of Greek paratroopers or U.S. troops together. We'll raid Krio Island and crush the conspiracy before it can get any worse."

"I'm afraid it's not that simple, David," Katz began. "We can't prove Krio and his group are involved in an insidious international plot. We can't even prove Sioris was murdered. The authorities will never agree to a raid without solid proof."

"Besides," James added, "Colonel Kostov is a pro. You can bet your ass he's got explosives wired to the lab just in case he has to destroy it in a hurry."

"Sure he'd destroy the evidence," McCarter said. "But he'd also get rid of the virus."

"On Krio Island." Katz nodded. "But don't forget this chemical was developed in the Soviet Union. If we destroy it here, that won't solve our problem. Or the threat facing the free world. We have to get a sample of the virus so our own scientists can analyze it. It's the only way we'll be able to defend ourselves against the virus if the Kremlin attempts to use it again in the future."

"Then that means Gary and Rafael will still have to go to the island," James said grimly.

"What's this?" McCarter raised his eyebrow.

Katz explained the plan to his British partner.

McCarter frowned. "I don't like it, Yakov," the

Englishman stated. "Sending them in there is too bloody dangerous. You know what happened to Sioris."

"Manning and Encizo have arranged to meet with Krio," Katz said. "Just a business meeting that should last only a few hours. The Greek isn't stupid, and neither is Kostov. They wouldn't do anything to a pair of so-called American businessmen, even if they suspected their visitors might be sent to spy on them."

"Tell that to Sioris," McCarter insisted. "They killed him, didn't they?"

"Sioris was on the island for almost twenty-four hours," Katz replied. "Krio clearly had no doubts about Sioris, but he can't be as certain about Manning and Encizo."

"That's an assumption," McCarter declared. "You *hope* Krio won't use the virus on them. Besides, what's the point? If Sioris didn't learn anything in an entire day on the island, why should we believe Gary and Rafael will do any better?"

"It does seem like an unnecessary risk, Yakov," James agreed.

"The value of firsthand information from two members of Phoenix Force is obvious," the Israeli told them. "Our people are better trained and more experienced than Sioris. We're the best in the business, or we wouldn't be part of Phoenix Force. The possible gain merits a degree of risk."

"You could order them not to go," James remarked.

"No, I can't," Katz replied. "Phoenix Force is a voluntary organization. We don't have to accept a mission, but when we do, we're committed to its success. The mission must be top priority. It is more important than our individual lives. If Manning and Encizo fail to meet with Krio, the Greek will suspect they were spies. He and Kostov will realize time is running out. They'll step up operations and possibly send out their agents before we can stop them.''

"But we've got to warn them about the starvation virus," James insisted. "Christ, Yakov. They've got a right to know what they're getting into."

"We'll warn them," Katz assured him. "If they want to cancel the meeting, they can. If they want to accept the risk and meet with Krio, that will be their decision, as well.''

"They'll do it, Katz," McCarter declared. "You know they will."

"I know." The Israeli nodded. "Meantime, we'd better plan our own strategy."

"And what the hell might that be?" the British vet asked.

"I think that will depend on what Mr. Krio and his syndicate decide to do next," the Israeli remarked with a shrug.

"What does that mean?" a confused Calvin James asked.

"Didn't you notice the gray sedan that followed us from the hospital?" Katz asked mildly.

"Yeah," the black man confirmed. "At the time I figured it was a backup team of Greek intel agents Draco hadn't bothered to tell us about...probably because he didn't trust us completely."

"I thought it might be something like that, too," Yakov stated. "Until David told us about Krio's crime syndicate. It seems Krio's people have already taken an interest in us.''

"Thank God," McCarter said with a wolfish grin. "That means we ought to see some bloody action soon."

"I knew that would make you feel better." Katz sighed.

9

Flight 909 from New York landed at the Athens airport thirty hours after the first three members of Phoenix Force had arrived in Greece. Gary Manning and Rafael Encizo deplaned and descended the ramp. Both men wore conservative, single-breasted suits and carried black attaché cases. They looked like a pair of junior executives on a business trip.

Of course, that was exactly what "Anthony Peters" and "Ramón Santos" were supposed to be. Manning and Encizo showed their forged passports to the customs officer and prepared to open their carryon luggage.

"Me-sighkoriti," the official said in an apologetic tone. "Excuse me, gentlemen, but your papers are not in order."

"There must be some mistake," Encizo protested in broken Greek. *"Parakalo.* Please, look again."

"Do not be difficult, Tongirio Santos," the official insisted. "You will both come with me. Now."

Encizo and Manning followed the customs man into a small office. They wondered if Brognola's people had made a mistake with the passports. Or was the customs man more than he appeared to be? If so, whose side was he on?

The office was sparsely furnished with a small

desk, two chairs, a telephone and some wall charts written in several languages, including English.

The official closed the door and bolted it. He turned to the foreigners and smiled. "Sorry to give you a bit of a start," the Greek said, his English containing a surprising cockney accent. "Working undercover is nerve-racking enough without an unexpected thing like this happening."

"Please explain yourself," Manning urged.

"No need to fret, guv," the customs man answered. "I'm Nikkos Papadopoulos, Greek Security Service. A Mr. Goldblum has a message for you blokes."

"I don't recognize the name." Manning frowned. "You know anybody named Goldblum, Santos?"

"Not that I can recall." Encizo shrugged. "Maybe you're talking to the wrong guys, Nikkos."

"Bleedin' careful, ain't you?" Nikkos grinned. "Goldblum wanted me to ask if you chaps tangled with any outlaw bikers or tiger sharks lately."

"Okay," Encizo said, offering his hand. "I guess those are a couple details the enemy couldn't have guessed, and nobody could have squeezed information out of our friend this quickly."

"Seemed like a tough old chap," Nikkos commented as he shook hands with the Cuban.

"To say the least," Manning confirmed.

"Bloody good," the Greek agent declared. "All right. I was told to give a message to the gent that speaks French and German."

"I'll take it," the Canadian replied.

"Righto." Nikkos nodded, taking a sealed envelope from his jacket. He handed it to Manning. "Wonder which language it's in."

Manning opened the envelope and extracted a note written by "Mr. Goldblum." The Canadian recognized Katz's handwriting. The letter was in both French and German, with a few English words sprinkled here and there. The multiple languages would make translating the message more difficult if it fell into enemy hands.

Cute, Katz, Manning thought sourly. Although the Canadian was fluent in all three languages, he still had to read the letter twice to be certain he understood it. The message told of what happened to Sioris and warned of the danger of the starvation virus on Krio Island. If Manning and Encizo wanted to back out, they would have to do so now.

"Excuse us for a minute," the Canadian told Nikkos.

Manning whispered the contents of the letter to Encizo. He kept his back turned to the Greek agent. The Canadian had worked with the deaf in college and could read lips in two languages. Manning never considered a conversation secure if someone could see his lips move.

"I say we continue our mission as planned," Encizo stated after Manning finished.

"I agree." The Canadian nodded. He turned to face Nikkos. "Okay. Secret conference over. Where can I destroy this message?"

"There's a loo over there," the Greek replied, indicating a door. "Just burn it and flush the ashes down the toilet, mate."

"Thanks, Nikkos," Manning said as he headed for the bathroom.

"Sure, guv." The Greek smiled. "We're all on the

same side, what? But you'd best hurry. Krio sent a couple gents with a car for you chaps. They're waitin' for you in the lounge.''

"The bastard doesn't believe in wasting time," Manning remarked.

"Only people," Encizo added with a shrug.

KRIO HAD SENT a limo for the "American businessmen." The driver was a burly man named Strabo, and he was accompanied by an English-speaking translator named Trypanis. The latter was a small, wiry man who wore horn-rimmed glasses and a linen suit. An artificial smile seemed frozen on his face as he introduced himself to Manning and Encizo.

Strabo, however, was a formidable figure. More than six feet tall, the chauffeur was built like an NFL lineman. Encizo noticed a layer of thick callus on the big knuckles of Strabo's first and second fingers. This suggested the driver had tempered his hands with a *makiwara*—a karate striking post. Encizo made a mental note of the fact that Strabo was potentially dangerous.

They loaded the baggage into the black limousine. The Phoenix Force pair and Trypanis climbed into the back of the vehicle. Strabo slid behind the steering wheel and started the motor.

"We'll drive to the Port of Piraeus," Trypanis explained. "From there we'll take a boat to Krio Island."

"Your boss certainly provides prompt transportation," Encizo remarked, drumming his fingers on the attaché case in his lap.

"Mr. Krio doesn't have many visitors," the Greek

translator stated. "But he believes in giving visitors first-class treatment. 'VIP,' as you Americans might say."

"That's flattering," Manning remarked. "And our company is eager to do business with Mr. Krio...providing we can come to agreeable terms."

"Mr. Krio is a reasonable man," Trypanis assured him. "I'm certain that can be accomplished."

"How long have you worked for him?" Encizo inquired.

"More than five years now," the Greek answered. "I'm just one of his accountants. Fortunately I speak English, so I was chosen to accompany Strabo."

"Do you live on the island?" the Cuban asked.

"Good heavens, no." Trypanis laughed. "My wife would hardly approve of that. I live in Athens, although I've spent some time on the island over the years. Wonderful place. I'm certain you'll find this to be the best business trip either of you have ever had."

"We hope it will be successful," Gary Manning admitted.

"It will be, Mr. Peters," Trypanis said. "If you'll glance outside, you'll notice we're passing by the Acropolis. Please enjoy the view."

Manning and Encizo turned to see one of the most famous collections of ancient monuments in the world. The remnants of numerous buildings, centuries old, surrounded the temple of Athena Parthenos. The Parthenon stood atop a hill, dominating the site.

"You should see the Parthenon at night with the floodlights trained on the temple," Trypanis remarked. "It looks like a glowing apparition from Mount Olympus. A beacon of Greek beauty and culture."

"It is impressive," Manning said sincerely.

The limousine passed several other famous sites. Trypanis continued to act as tour guide. Obviously this was all part of a plan to impress the VIP guests from America. Strabo drove the limo at a moderate speed and cruised by as many points of interest as possible. Manning and Encizo simply enjoyed the tour and tried to relax before they had to enter the lion's den known as Krio Island.

Eventually the limo pulled onto Pireos Street and headed for the Port of Piraeus. Strabo drove on to Pasalimani Harbor, where hundreds of yachts were tied up at the piers. The car cruised slowly down the dock and finally pulled to a halt.

Trypanis smiled and pointed at one of the larger vessels. "And there's our ride," he announced.

The yacht Trypanis referred to was a fifty-foot-long ketch with the legend *Argo* painted on the transom. A figure dressed in a white silk shirt and matching duck trousers stood on the deck at the port quarter. The man cheerfully smiled and waved at Encizo and Manning. They recognized him from a photograph they had seen during the briefing that began their mission.

The man was Dimitri Krio.

The Greek tycoon was only five and a half feet tall, but his straight posture and tailored clothing created the illusion of additional height. His belly was thick with a round stomach. The breeze ruffled Krio's silver hair as he displayed his perfect white teeth in a crocodile smile.

"Kalispera," Krio greeted them. "Welcome, gentlemen. Please come aboard."

Manning, Encizo and Trypanis obliged. Strabo placed the luggage on board and returned to the limousine. Krio shouted an order in Greek to a pair of muscular young crew members, and they nodded and hurried to the bridge.

The tycoon led his guests to a set of deck chairs beneath the shade of a colorful canopy. Milo, Krio's valet, immediately brought them a bottle of champagne in a bucket of ice and a tray with four glasses.

"Shall we drink a toast to success, wealth and all the other good things in life?" Krio inquired as Milo popped the cork from the bottle.

"Can't argue with that," Manning replied. "Your hospitality is overwhelming, Mr. Krio."

"Call me 'Dimitri.'" The Greek smiled. "We are going to be friends, so let us not stand on formalities."

The yacht cruised smoothly away from the dock and headed into the bay. Milo poured the champagne.

Krio raised his glass to salute Manning and Encizo. "I trust you had a pleasant trip, gentlemen," he commented, sipping his wine.

"Very pleasant," Encizo assured him. "Thanks to Mr. Trypanis's tour of Athens."

"Kalo," the tycoon declared. "Good. I like to make my friends happy. I am glad things are going well. Ah! Look at that sunset! Beautiful, is it not?"

The great orange sphere seemed to melt into the horizon. A prism effect caused a collage of color to splash across the Mediterranean. The lights were incredible, brilliant, alive and fascinating.

"We didn't realize it was getting so late," Manning remarked. "Guess we should have checked into the hotel and arranged to meet you in the morning."

"Do not be silly, Anthony." Krio laughed. "You are Anthony, correct? Well, you and Ramón will stay at my house tonight. Everything is arranged. I promise we will take good care of you both."

"You're too kind," Manning said. He managed a smile, although a hard cold knot had formed in the pit of his stomach.

10

Krio Island was too small to appear on most maps of the Greek islands. From recon photos, Manning and Encizo knew it to be only seven miles long, with a narrow strip of beach forming a sandy belt around the circumference. Several buildings protruded from the inland area like concrete knuckles on a giant fist.

The island seemed sinister to Gary Manning and Rafael Encizo. Perhaps this was due to the shadows of twilight or because they realized the place was an enemy stronghold. Neither man relished the idea of spending the night on Krio Island.

Yet their host remained charming and pleasant. Dimitri Krio chatted with his guests in a friendly manner while the crew docked the *Argo* in a small yacht harbor. Two security guards dressed in khaki uniforms met the boat. They carried walkie-talkies and holstered pistols on their Sam Browne belts.

"I've prepared two guest rooms for you," Krio told Manning and Encizo. "I'll have the security men carry up your luggage."

"Is security a problem on the island, Dimitri?" Encizo inquired.

"Not really," the tycoon answered. "Just precaution. A man with my success and wealth is bound to be a target one way or the other. Critics are just an annoyance. Thieves, kidnappers and terrorists are another matter.''

"You're wise to take precautions," the Cuban said. "Especially since international terrorism has increased to such an alarming level."

"Yes." Krio sighed. "It's terrible. Isn't it?"

The tycoon's house was a mansion that reflected a variety of architectural styles. The front steps were marble and the pediment was supported by Doric columns. The house itself appeared to be made of white brick and featured Islamic-style windows with a trefoil arch.

"You named your boat the *Argo*," Encizo commented as they followed Krio inside the house. "Wasn't that the ship Jason sailed during his quest for the Golden Fleece?"

They entered a spacious hallway complete with a red carpet, miniature palm trees in onyx pots and Hellenistic urns. A great marble staircase ascended to the next story.

"So you're familiar with Greek mythology, Ramón?" Krio remarked. "You're right, of course. Isn't every man seeking a 'Golden Fleece' of one kind or another?"

"I wouldn't think you'd have any fleece left to quest for, Dimitri," Manning commented. "You're already rich, influential and powerful. What more could you want?"

"More of the same." Krio smiled. "What else?"

DINNER WAS A GOURMET'S DREAM. The *orekika*, or hors d'oeuvres, consisted of salad, cheese and *kalamari* squid. This was followed by *kakavia* soup, which Manning noted tasted similar to French bouillabaisse. The main course featured zucchini, artichokes, boiled lobster and shish kebab.

"Being Americans you're probably accustomed to eating early in the evening," Krio began. "But in Greece we usually have dinner sometime after eight o'clock."

"This meal would be superb at any hour," Manning assured him. "Say, what sort of meat is this on the shish kebab?"

"*Kokkoretsi*," Krio replied. "A favorite among Greek country folk."

"It's delicious," the Canadian declared.

"I'm glad you like it." The Greek smiled. "So many Americans object to lamb entrails."

Manning dropped his fork and uttered an abrupt cough.

"Dimitri," Encizo said quickly, trying to distract Krio's attention from the distressed Manning. "Do you do much business with Yugoslavia?"

"Of course," Krio answered. "And Bulgaria, as well. Why, do you find trading with Communists distasteful?"

"Well, our corporation doesn't have a current import-export connection with either country." The Cuban shrugged.

"And naturally they want to tap into a source," Krio said with approval. "That's a wise move. Politics shouldn't get in the way of making a profit. Bulgaria is more promising a source for international trade than most Westerners realize. Did you know the metallurgical combine at Kremikovtsi is among the largest iron-and-steel plants in the world? The

Bulgarians produce a tremendous amount of machinery. They need connections to other countries in order to export these goods.''

"I thought the Bulgarians shipped most of their products to the Soviet Union,'' Manning remarked.

"They do,'' the Greek confirmed. "But Bulgaria also trades with non-Communist countries. Both the United States and Greece have been reluctant to deal with Bulgaria. Yet your government has trade with the Russians. America sells grain to the Soviet Union, but it doesn't want to do business with Bulgaria.''

Krio sipped some wine and continued. "For Greece not to deal with Bulgaria is even more absurd. The Bulgarians export more goods to France and Japan than to Greece. Doesn't it make sense to trade with your neighbors and try to get along with them?''

"Bulgaria doesn't get along very well with some of its neighbors,'' the Canadian commented. "Turkey and Yugoslavia aren't exactly chummy with Bulgaria.''

"Turkey and Greece aren't terribly close, either,'' Krio stated. "Yugoslavia and Bulgaria are still quarreling about that Macedonian business. Such petty political nonsense shouldn't get in the way of businessmen like us. However, you must be tired after such a long journey. May I suggest we all get a good night's sleep and tackle business once more in the morning?''

"That sounds fine, Dimitri,'' Encizo agreed.

"Good.'' The Greek nodded. "I'll tell Milo to serve dessert and coffee. That is, unless Anthony would care for some more *kokkoretsi*.''

"Uh...thanks," Manning replied. "But I think I've had enough."

GARY MANNING'S QUARTERS were neat and pleasant. In addition to a bed, closet and bathroom, the room also featured a chest of drawers with mirror, a desk, chairs and a radio.

The Canadian found his suitcase and valise at the foot of the bed. He hummed tunelessly as he set his suitcase on the bureau. Manning unlocked the case and opened it, covering the mirror with the lid. The suitcase would block the view of anyone who might be spying on him via a two-way mirror.

Of course, the room was probably bugged. He would have to be careful about what sort of sounds he made until he could sweep for electronic listening devices.

Manning examined the contents of his suitcase. He was not surprised to discover his shirts were folded differently from when he packed them and his shaving kit was at a different angle. Krio's people had searched his luggage. They had done a professional job. Few observers would have noticed anything had been disturbed. Had they found anything to suggest "Anthony Peters" was more than he appeared to be?

A knock on the door startled the Canadian. His first instinct was to close the suitcase, but he controlled the impulse. Manning quickly pulled a drawer open and tossed two shirts into it.

"Come in," he invited. *"Ehlate mesa."*

Manning loosened his necktie as he headed for the door. It opened before he could reach the knob. The

Canadian stared at his unexpected visitor, stunned by what he saw.

She was beautiful. A tall, shapely woman with long black hair and emerald green eyes. Full lips formed a wide smile on her alabaster face. The woman glided into the room and gently closed the door. "My name is Melina," she announced. "I'm here to make certain your night is a pleasant one."

"Oh," Manning said, because he could not think of a better reply. "That's not necessary."

"You don't like me?" Melina frowned. "If you don't think you'd enjoy going to bed with me, tell me what kind of woman you would rather have."

"Christ," the Canadian muttered. Krio *really* believed in taking care of his guests.

"Perhaps you don't like women," Melina remarked. "Would you rather have a man?"

"No," Manning replied firmly.

"I am glad of that," she purred as she moved closer. "It would be a pity if a handsome man like you did not desire women."

"That's a very nice compliment, Melina," the Canadian said. "And you are a very beautiful and desirable woman, but I can't—"

"Have you heard how wild and passionate Greek women can be?" Melina inquired, slipping her arms around his neck. "It's true. I'll prove it if you let me."

"I. . . ." Manning tried to think about something besides the lovely woman who pressed her breasts against his chest. "I'm married."

"But your wife is still in America," Melina whispered. "And I am here with you."

She crushed her mouth against his. Manning embraced the woman, unable to resist the temptation. He returned her kiss, running his tongue along her teeth and up to the roof of her mouth. Melina slid a hand down his torso. Her fingers stroked the stiff bulge at his crotch.

"Come, Anthony," the woman crooned. "Let us have a good time."

"I'm really tired," Manning gasped as Melina squeezed his rigid member.

"You're not *that* tired," she insisted.

"Well." The Canadian sighed. "Maybe you're right about that."

The things I have to do for Phoenix Force, Manning thought as he removed his jacket.

11

"I don't think I like being bait, Mr. Goldblum," Manos Draco confessed as he drove his Volkswagen Rabbit onto Navarinou Street.

"Neither do I," Yakov Katzenelenbogen agreed. "But Krio's agents are already aware we're in Athens, so we can't operate without their knowledge, anyway."

"We could have tried some sort of disguise," the one-eyed Greek intel man muttered. He glanced about at the streetlights and the neon signs that branded the night.

"There are a limited number of ways to alter one's appearance," Katz stated. "None of them is foolproof. Sometimes disguises work. Sometimes they don't. Believe me, I speak from personal experience."

"At times like these I wish I still had Saint Christopher in my car." Draco sighed.

Katz mulled over the discussion he, James and McCarter had had with the Greek security officer and Kalvo, the CIA case officer. No one was delighted about trying to lure the enemy into making the next move, but it appeared he, James and Draco had already been "burned"—their covers exposed to the other side. The same might be true about McCarter,

Kalvo and other members of Greek intel involved, Katz thought.

That was the reason he had a messenger deliver a note to Manning and Encizo at the airport. Until the pair returned from Krio Island, the others would have to deal with the tycoon's syndicate in Athens. A lure seemed the only logical choice of action.

A briefcase on the floor between his feet contained a compact Uzi submachine gun with two spare magazines. He noticed that Draco had a NATO Sumak-9 subgun in the back seat. A 9mm blow-back weapon similar to the American M-3, the Sumak-9 could unleash a death spray that could cut a man in half.

In addition to the submachine guns, both men were armed with pistols. Katz carried a SIG-Sauer P-226 in shoulder leather under his right arm. An excellent double-action autoloader, the P-226 could fire off fifteen rounds of 9mm hollowpoints as smoothly as a hot needle passes through butter. The Israeli also carried a .380 Astra Constable in a pancake holster at the small of his back for a holdout piece. Draco had a 9mm FN Browning automatic and a fighting dagger strapped to his right ankle.

Katz pressed the transmit button to a communicator. "Nighthawk One to Nighthawk Two. Over," he spoke into the radio.

"Nighthawk Two," the voice of David McCarter replied. "Read you fine, Nighthawk One. Over."

"Any news? Over."

"Just a big gray shadow," the Briton answered. "He's about four cars behind you, but tagging along. No doubt about that. Over."

"Don't get lost, Nighthawk Two."

"Stay tuned to this channel for further developments," McCarter said, imitating a stuffy BBC announcer.

"Over and out." Katz ended transmission.

McCarter, James and Kalvo were following in another vehicle to back up Katz and Draco in an emergency. The Briton's report warned Katz that the lure had worked. They were being tailed. Probably by the same gray sedan Katz had noticed earlier in the day.

"What do we do now?" Draco inquired. His knuckles jutted from his fists as he clenched the steering wheel harder.

"We try to pick the battleground," Katz replied. "Let's lead the tail to someplace remote. We don't want to endanger more people than we have to."

"A remote area in Athens?" The Greek agent groaned. "This city has a population of more than eight hundred fifty thousand people, not including tourists."

"Get us out of Athens if you have to," the Phoenix Force commander instructed. "Or possibly to a construction site or a limestone quarry. Anyplace there won't be a bunch of civilians to worry about."

"I'll try." Draco sighed. "But I can't—"

Suddenly a large beer truck pulled out of an alley in front of the Rabbit. Draco cursed and stomped the brake pedal. The car skidded forward and nearly nose-dived into the side of the larger vehicle.

"Down!" Katz shouted when he saw the tarp cover fly back from the rear of the truck.

Draco heeded the Israeli's advice just in time. A shotgun bellowed. The windshield of the VW exploded when a burst of buckshot crashed into it. Shattered glass showered Katz and Draco as they huddled on the floor of the car.

Pedestrians screamed in terror. A tour bus swerved away from the beer truck and rammed into a lamppost. A kid on a moped steered his bike onto the sidewalk. He leaped off the two-wheeler before it came to a full stop. The kid hit the pavement, rolled and dashed to the entrance of a coffee shop for cover.

"Theos!" Draco gasped. "They set up an ambush!"

"I noticed," Katz said dryly as he popped open the door on the passenger's side. "Stay down."

Another shotgun blast ripped into the backrest of the front seat. Katz tried to ignore the fearsome destruction caused by the buckshot. If he thought about what the devastating pellets could do to human flesh, he might hesitate. To hesitate was to die.

Motivated by the will to survive and highly developed reflexes, honed by years of experience in combat, the Israeli tumbled from the car. The hook at the end of his right arm gripped the handle of the briefcase. Katz crouched behind the open car door, using it for cover as he drew the SIG-Sauer and flicked off the safety catch.

A high velocity bullet slapped into the door. Katz heard the sharp crack of a pistol as the slug pierced the metal skin.

Katz heard another shotgun blast smash into the hood of the Volkswagen. He glanced inside to see if Draco had been hit. A figure appeared at the window by the driver's seat and aimed a revolver at Draco.

The battle-edged Israeli snap-aimed and triggered

his P-226. The SIG-Sauer snarled twice. Two 9mm rounds punched through the windowpane. The gunman's face was transformed into a crimson pulp. The would-be assassin slumped from view.

A bullet struck the frame of the car two inches above Katz's head. The Israeli's heart raced as he whirled to face the terrorist who emerged from the alley.

The killer aimed a Hungarian 9mm Walam pistol at Yakov. Katz fired the SIG-Sauer. The gunman doubled up when a slug drilled into his stomach. The Walam spat fire, but the muzzle was pointed at the pavement. A bullet whined as it ricocheted off concrete. Katz blasted another parabellum round through the top of his opponent's bowed head.

Another shotgun volley peppered the front of the VW. Katz scrambled to the rear of the vehicle and dropped to one knee. He popped open his briefcase and quickly extracted the Uzi. The Israeli shoved the P-226 into his belt and worked the bolt of the subgun to chamber a round.

Katz rose up and fired a salvo of full-auto brimstone at the truck. Uzi slugs chopped into the chest of the shotgunner positioned at the back of the beer truck. The force of the 9mm hornet swarm sent the gunman's corpse hurtling backward into a column of wooden kegs.

A second figure, also armed with a double-barreled, sawed-off shotgun, hastily pointed his weapon at Katz. The Phoenix Force pro had already ducked low before the shotgun belched a spray of deadly buckshot. Pellets rang against metal and concrete, but none struck flesh.

The shotgunner shuffled to a better position and trained his scattergun on Katz. Manos Draco suddenly thrust his arm through the shot-out windshield. He aimed the Browning pistol in his fist and fired twice. The enemy gunman's head snapped backward as one of the 115-grain projectiles sizzled through bone and brain.

Panic-stricken, the driver of the truck stomped on the gas pedal. The big vehicle lurched forward. The nose of the truck slammed into the side of the disabled tour bus. Vacationers inside shrieked when the frame of the bus caved in.

The door to the cab of the truck opened. Katz saw the frightened driver dash from the enemy vehicle. The terrorist blindly fired a pistol at the VW as he ran. The Israeli aimed low and triggered the Uzi.

A salvo of 9mm slugs sliced into the fleeing man's legs. Flesh and muscle turned into jelly. Bone shattered. The terrorist screamed as he tumbled headlong to the pavement.

Katz rushed forward, holding his Uzi ready in case more enemies still lurked in the shadows. He moved to the wounded man. The guy's neck rested along the curb. A scarlet pool surrounded his broken skull.

"Is he the last one?" Draco asked as he jogged to Katz's side.

"For now," the Israeli replied grimly. "But this is just the beginning, my friend."

12

Melina nudged Gary Manning. The Canadian uttered an involuntary grunt and rolled over onto his back. He did not open his eyes, and his breathing remained steady. Melina gradually slid out from under the bed sheets and off the mattress.

Naked, she padded barefoot across to the foot of the bed and picked up her discarded purse. She continued to watch Manning. She had been trained to recognize the telltale signs of a person pretending to be asleep.

Muscles relaxed during slumber. A faker was usually too tense; the eyelids were closed too firmly, and breathing remained regular, but not too steady. Manning did not appear to be faking.

Melina smiled. Anthony Peters, if that was indeed his real name, had been good in bed. He was gentle during foreplay and passionate while making love. His sexual endurance startled the woman. Melina could not recall enjoying sex with a stranger before. Seduction was part of her job, but she had never had an orgasm while "working" until that night. The stranger was quite a man.

Manning's attitude seemed genuine. He had been slightly awkward until he surrendered to lust. Yet Melina was not certain the man was what he claimed to be. He was very muscular for a business executive. But some Americans were health fanatics who dieted and exercised daily.

The numerous scars on his superb physique disturbed Melina. He had told her they were old war wounds from the Vietnam conflict. Perhaps that was true, but Melina learned long ago not to believe anything a man said.

What bothered her the most, however, was the fact that Manning did not wear a wedding ring. Yet he had been reluctant to sleep with her because he claimed he was married.

She opened her purse and removed a tiny .25-caliber Beretta automatic. Melina snapped off the safety and pointed the pistol at Manning. He still did not stir.

"CIA pig," she whispered. "I'm going to kill you."

Melina drew closer and aimed the Beretta at the sleeping head. Manning did not respond to the threat. His eyes remained lightly closed; his breathing did not increase. Melina smiled. Satisfied he was truly asleep, she lowered the pistol.

The woman returned to the foot of the bed. She knelt beside the bundle of clothing that she and Manning had stripped off before they'd made love. Melina kept the .25 auto in her fist as she examined Manning's suit jacket.

She probed the fabric with her fingertips, trusting touch more than sight in the dim light. The woman checked the contents of pockets. Passport, two fountains pens, a handkerchief, plane ticket, but nothing unusual. She felt for evidence of anything sewed into the cloth itself. Still nothing.

Then she examined his trousers. Wallet, spare

change, some keys attached to a small pocket flashlight. The wallet contained money, credit cards and a few photographs of a middle-aged couple and a younger woman. These were, in fact, pictures of Manning's parents and his ex-wife Lorraine.

Melina thought she had discovered something suspicious when she felt a zipper on the inside of Manning's belt. She opened it to find two hundred-dollar bills inside. Melina zipped the money belt shut and checked Manning's shoes. There was nothing hidden inside, and the heels were not hollow.

Melina picked up her dress and shoes. She rose and smiled at the quiet figure lying in the bed. Maybe Anthony Peters was just who he claimed to be after all. She hoped so for his sake.

The woman slipped into her dress and returned the Beretta to her purse. She carried her shoes to the door. Melina opened it and silently left the room.

GARY MANNING STARED at the luminous dial of the Seiko wristwatch on the nightstand beside him. He waited five minutes to be certain Melina had not decided to make a quick check to see if he was still in the bed. The Canadian sat up and breathed deeply, drawing air through his nostrils slowly and exhaling through his mouth.

The late Keio Ohara had taught him *zazen* breath control. The Japanese meditation technique was useful in dealing with tension and stress. Manning needed it now. Pretending to be asleep had not been easy, especially when the woman had aimed a gun at his head and said she was going to kill him.

Of course, the threat had been only a test. If Krio

wanted Manning dead, he would not have bothered playing games. Melina had been sent only to search the Canadian's clothing. Others had already checked out his luggage.

Yet Manning and Encizo were still in considerable danger. Krio was the supreme ruler on the island. He could order their execution anytime he wanted. Colonel Kostov was also somewhere on the island. The veteran Bulgarian agent would know all about methods employed to force men to talk. Torture, truth serum, sleep deprivation, whatever it took to break a man, Kostov would be familiar with it.

Worse, the Phoenix Force pair may have already been marked for death. They did not know how the mysterious starvation chemical worked. It could have been in their food, or smeared on the surface of their wineglasses. If it could be turned into a mist, it might have been sprayed into the guest rooms and inhaled.

Keep worrying about it and you'll give yourself stomachaches for sure, Manning told himself. He climbed out of bed. Time to get back to work.

He padded over to his clothes and found his penlight. The Canadian did not want to turn on the lamp; a light in the window might be noticed by someone outside. Then he opened his wallet and removed a plastic credit card. The VISA card was a forgery printed in the name of Anthony Peters. Yet it was more than just a prop for Manning's false identity. The Canadian snapped off the bottom of the card and moved to his open suitcase.

He removed the contents from the luggage and ripped the lining to slip the plastic strip from the broken card into a hidden slot. The strip was actually a "flat key." The numbers of the expiration date for the card activated a computer-programmed tumbler. Manning heard a dull click and pulled open the lid to a secret compartment built into the case.

The Canadian did not like gadgets. "Bond-foolery," he often called them. But the computerized false bottom to the suitcase had worked well enough. The compartment was lined with a thin lead shield to hide detection from X rays. It had fooled customs and, apparently, Krio's people, as well.

Manning removed the secret contents of the compartment. First he extracted a narrow strip of Composition Four wrapped in brown paper. Manning liked C-4 for what it was, a very stable yet extremely potent plastic explosive. He set the C-4 on the counter and took a small plastic box from the compartment.

He pried it open and removed a diminutive Sterling Model 302 automatic. Only thirteen ounces and less than five inches long, the Sterling held six rounds of .22 Long Rifle ammunition.

The last objects Manning took from the compartment were a pair of infrared goggles and a tiny metal packet slightly larger than a book of matches. A metal prong, similar to a tuning fork, protruded from the little packet. The odd contraption was a "bug sweeper," for detecting electronic listening devices.

Manning decided to see to his weaponry first. He unzipped the money belt and removed the two bills. Then he unwrapped the C-4 and inserted the plastic explosive into the belt.

Suddenly the door opened. The Canadian snatched up the little Sterling pistol. Rafael Encizo stood in the doorway, shaking his head. He jerked a thumb over his shoulder to indicate he wanted to speak to Manning in the hall. The Canadian nodded and walked softly to the door.

"I thought you'd never get your ass in gear, damn it," the Cuban complained when Manning joined him in the corridor.

"Sorry," Manning replied. "But they sent a woman to my room, and I had to wait until she left."

"They sent one to me, too." Encizo shrugged. "Come on. I'll introduce you to her."

The Canadian followed Encizo to another guest room. A radio was playing softly, and a naked woman lay on the bed, snoring. Manning looked at Encizo. His puzzled expression amused the Cuban.

"Talk quietly," Encizo whispered. "The radio is playing next to a bug. See how busy I've been while you were still sitting around naked?"

"What about the woman?" Manning asked.

"I guess I was just too much man for the poor thing to handle," Encizo grinned.

"Rafael . . ." Manning began sharply.

"Okay." The Cuban sighed. "If you must know, I had her bring us a bottle of wine and I slipped her a little chlorpromazine. She'll be out for at least two hours."

"You ready to take a midnight stroll?" Manning asked.

"I've *been* ready for half an hour," the Cuban complained.

Both men had donned black trousers and matching turtleneck shirts and rubber-soled shoes. Encizo was also armed with a tiny Sterling autoloader and carried a Gerber Mark I fighting dagger in a sheath at the small of his back.

"I hope we don't have to use any of this hardware tonight," the Cuban remarked. "Just as soon make a nice quiet recon of the island and leave here in the morning without Krio and company being aware we cased this place."

"Maybe we'll be lucky," the Canadian shrugged.

"We have been so far," Encizo sighed. "That's what worries me. Everything has gone *too* well."

"Jesus," Manning muttered, "you're a cynic."

"I'm more of a realist than a cynic," Encizo replied. "Realistically I know something *always* goes wrong on a mission."

"You've been hanging around McCarter too much," Manning commented. "Let's get to our mission before sunrise. Okay?"

13

"We're still on their arse," David McCarter spoke into his transceiver.

McCarter referred to the gray sedan that had shadowed Katz and Draco before their VW Rabbit was ambushed. When the fireworks erupted the sedan kept going. Since McCarter, James and Paul Kalvo arrived too late to help their commander in the firefight, they continued to pursue the big gray car.

"Careful, Nighthawk Two," Katz's voice urged. "They obviously have a radio link with other terrorists, or they couldn't have arranged an ambush. Over."

"We'll bear that in mind, mate," the Briton agreed. "You chaps take care, too. Over and out."

Paul Kalvo glanced in the rearview mirror as he drove the Fiat. The CIA man clucked his tongue with disgust when he saw McCarter in the back seat. The mission-toughened vet was grinning like a kid at Christmas as he opened a briefcase to examine his Ingram machine pistol.

Kalvo was no more pleased by the conduct of Calvin James, who sat in the front seat beside him. The CIA case officer would never have admitted he was prejudiced against blacks, but that was one reason he did not like James. Another reason was because the man was cheerfully humming to himself as he drew the blade of a G-96 Jet-Aer fighting dagger along a sharpening steel.

"I want you both to know I'm not going to write a favorable report about this business," Kalvo warned.

"Shee-it," James replied, testing the double-edged blade of his knife with a thumb. "What you wanna get on our case for, man?"

He used jive because he realized it bothered Kalvo. You don't like us, James thought. So fuck you. He slipped the G-96 into a sheath under his right arm. The scabbard was attached to a Jackass Leather rig, which included a shoulder holster for the Colt Commander under his left arm.

"You three hotshots are all too trigger happy," the CIA man snapped. "Look at what happened back there! A gun battle in the middle of goddamn Athens—and right out in the streets, too! Is that what you people call keeping a low profile?"

"We call it staying alive, you silly bastard," said an impatient McCarter. "Or would you have been happier if Goldblum and Draco had been killed?"

"Chasing after these damn gangsters is asking for trouble," Kalvo insisted.

"We've already got trouble," James said bluntly. "That's why we're here. To take care of a problem before it turns into an international disaster."

"You people are too—"

"Listen, Kalvo," McCarter interrupted, "just follow that bloody sedan. If you let those bastards get away you'll have a lot more to worry about than the Company's public relations in Greece."

"Heads up!" James announced eagerly. "See what I see?"

The sedan had pulled in front of a small building. Neither James nor McCarter could read the legend above the door, but the tinted windows and a crude painting of a grinning mermaid with enormous breasts suggested the place was a tavern. However, a big black limousine parked at the curb indicated the bar attracted a rather exclusive clientele.

"Drive past the place," James instructed. "Don't speed up or slow down, and don't stare at the bastards...."

"Look, Johnson," Kalvo snapped. "I know my job. I'm not a goddamn amateur."

"Glad you told us," McCarter muttered.

Kalvo drove past the tavern. They managed to get a glimpse of the two gangsters who emerged from the sedan. One was a tall man dressed in a white suit, black shirt and a fedora. His companion was a stocky character clad in a brown leather jacket and a black wool cap.

"Did you see those nitwits?" James chuckled. "They looked like something out of the late show."

"Don't laugh," Kalvo said sternly as he continued to drive down the street. "I recognized the guy in the suit from his mug shot in our files. He's Kosta Chrysostomos. The goon with him is probably Constantine Mercouri."

"We're from out of town, remember?" McCarter stated. "What's special about those blokes?"

"The police suspect they're professional killers," the CIA man replied. "They've both got a history of violence. Several arrests. No convictions. Now they're working for Theo Xerxes. The cops think Xerxes is Mr. Big, sort of a Greek version of the Godfather. We've found out the real *cappo* is Krio. Xerxes is just his commander here in Athens.''

"Well, I'll be damned," James remarked. "You've done your homework on this subject, pal."

"We've been interested in Krio's connection with organized crime for some time," Kalvo admitted.

"Oh?" James raised his eyebrows. "You mean, before this business with the Bulgarians and the terrorists?"

"Yeah," the CIA man said awkwardly. "Well, I suppose it can't hurt to tell you about it now. You see, we were gathering information about Krio's syndicate in order to nail him on conspiracy charges for the various crimes committed by Xerxes and his people. Then the CIA, working with the Greek authorities, would offer Krio amnesty if he'd spill his guts about his involvement with the Communists. If he'd give us enough information about the Reds' plans in the Mediterranean region, we'd see to it he got relocated in Switzerland.''

"Don't be embarrassed." McCarter laughed. "Blackmail and making deals is part of your trade. So is killing people from time to time. Which reminds me, did you bring along a gun?"

"A .38 snubnose revolver," Kalvo replied. "But I've never shot anyone. I didn't get into the Company in order to kill people."

"Terrorists aren't people," McCarter told him. "They're cockroaches that walk upright."

"You don't intend to just march into the tavern and start shooting?" the CIA man stared at McCarter.

"Of course not," James assured him. "Terrorists don't care about killing innocent people, but we do."

"Not very likely anybody in there is innocent." McCarter shrugged. "Only three cars parked in front of the place. All of them look pretty expensive, too. I'll lay odds everybody in there is a gangster."

"What about the bartender?" James asked.

"He's probably a syndicate man, too," Kalvo stated. "The tavern is a front set up by Xerxes. He's got them all over Athens. Didn't you notice the sign in the window? It means the place is closed."

"So the hoods are having a private get-together tonight." McCarter smiled. "Now let's just figure out how we're going to crash their party."

PAUL KALVO HALF DRAGGED, half carried David Mc-Carter to the front door of the Neroyinka Tavern. McCarter held both arms against his abdomen and bowed his head as if suffering from severe stomach pains.

"This isn't going to work, Miller," Kalvo whispered through clenched teeth.

"We can't wait for reinforcements to get here," McCarter whispered back. "The bastards might get away. We have to do it this way."

"But—"

"Quiet," McCarter rasped. "We're almost at the bleedin' door."

Kalvo knocked on the panel. The sound of shoe leather on linoleum was the only reply from within the tavern. McCarter began to moan. Kalvo knocked harder.

"Voitha'oh!" he shouted. "Help! There's been an accident!"

"Go away!" a voice snapped in curt Greek from the opposite side of the door.

"Parakalo," Kalvo insisted. "Please, I told you we need help. I've got an injured man...."

"That is not our problem," the voice snarled. "This isn't a hospital."

"Just let us use your telephone," Kalvo pleaded.

"Go pester someone else," the surly Greek inside the tavern answered. "Unless you want us to shoot your friend to put him out of his misery."

Laughter followed. McCarter did not understand the conversation, but the sound of the laughter was hardly encouraging. The men inside seemed to be amused by rejecting aid to an injured man. McCarter tried to guess how many voices were laughing. No less than three, he figured. Probably more.

"Sta'sis!" a voice snapped a command. The laughter ceased abruptly.

McCarter and Kalvo heard a bolt slide back. The door opened, and the tall man dressed in a white suit appeared. He offered them an artificial smile.

"I apologize for my friend," Chrysostomos told them. "He is overconcerned about crime in Athens. What seems to be wrong with your friend?"

"Car accident," Kalvo replied. "I think his ribs are broken."

"I see." The gangster nodded. "Please come in."

McCarter and Kalvo entered the tavern. The barroom contained simple wooden furniture. The walls were decorated with an assortment of fishnets, starfish and whaling harpoons. Stools surrounded circular tables, and a jukebox, which appeared to be at least twenty years old, sat in one corner of the room.

The bar was a plain counter, with a heavy-set bald man stationed behind it.

Six men were seated at the tables. They varied in age and general appearance, but all seemed apprehensive about the unexpected visitors. Their eyes remained fixed on McCarter and Kalvo. Muscles tensed in their faces. Three of them slipped their hands inside jackets.

Kosta Chrysostomos closed the door. He then held up a .380 Beretta automatic in his right fist. A 7-inch sound suppressor was attached to the muzzle. The gangster aimed his weapon at Kalvo. "You police must think we're very stupid, eh?" Chrysostomos remarked.

" 'Police'?" Kalvo gasped. "We are not policemen. My friend and I—"

"If you're not police, that's too bad." Chrysostomos shrugged. "If you are police, then this is part of a trap. Either way, you two have to die."

David McCarter suddenly exploded into action. He adroitly tripped Paul Kalvo and shoved the CIA man with his left hand to send Kalvo to the floor. The warrior's right hand reflexively drew his Browning Hi-Power from the Bianchi holster under his arm as he threw himself to the linoleum, as well.

Chrysostomos was caught off guard by McCarter's tactic. The unexpected movement caused him to instinctively trigger his Beretta. The silenced pistol coughed harshly, and a .380 slug smashed into the door.

McCarter fired his first shot before he hit the floor. Two decades of pistol shooting and years of combat experience did the rest. Chrysostomos screamed as a

115-grain hollowpoint projectile ripped into his chest.

The Browning barked again and a second 9mm bullet struck Chrysostomos in the side of the face. The slug split his cheekbone and drilled an upward path to the gangster's brain. Kosta Chrysostomos's criminal career came to an abrupt and final end.

Before Chrysostomos's corpse fell, the other Greek hoods drew their weapons and opened fire. Lead missiles splintered floorboards and chipped wood from the legs of the table and stool that McCarter had rolled behind.

Adrenaline pumped through the SAS vet's veins. Excitement overcame fear. McCarter hardly noticed the enemy bullets that struck only inches from his prone figure. Wooden shards bit into the commando's hands, but this did not prevent him from aiming the Browning at the closest gangster.

He squeezed the trigger. The hood's head recoiled violently when a parabellum round nailed him in the forehead. Another Greek buttonman fired a 7.65mm Model 57 pistol at McCarter. The diminutive bullet found its target and pierced flesh, to burn a furrow through the Briton's right triceps.

"Bloody hell," McCarter gritted through clenched teeth as he fired back at his assailant.

The gunman shrieked. He dropped his Yugoslavian autoloader and doubled up with a 9mm slug buried in his large intestine. McCarter fired two more rounds into the wounded man's upper torso. A third Greek killer collapsed to the floor, but more remained to avenge their slain comrades.

A side entrance to the Neroyinka burst open as

Calvin James kicked in the door and charged across the threshold. He held a Smith & Wesson Model 76 submachine gun in his fists.

The black commando instantly evaluated the situation with a professional glance. Two syndicate goons had turned over a table for cover as they fired pistols at McCarter and Kalvo. Another Greek gangster had moved to the cover of a pillar and aimed a revolver at the Briton's position. The bartender took a double-barreled shotgun from under his counter and prepared to join the battle, as well.

James aimed his M-76 and caressed the trigger. A 3-round burst of 9mm hail slashed into the spine of the hood stationed behind the pillar. The man screamed as bullets shattered his backbone and severed his spinal cord. Skin was scraped from his face as he slid down the pillar to the floor.

The bartender swung his shotgun toward James, but the black man had already selected him for his next target. The S&W chatterbox rattled out a curt metallic song of death. Two parabellum rounds tore into the bartender's upper chest. A third delivered a very messy tracheotomy as it punched through the hollow of his throat. The bartender dropped his scattergun and clutched both hands to his bullet-gouged neck. Then his eyes rolled toward the ceiling and he collapsed behind the bar.

The two killers stationed behind the table shelter heard the roar of James's submachine gun. The syndicate triggermen quickly turned their attention toward the black commando. In doing so, they made a fatal mistake—they turned their backs to Paul Kalvo.

The CIA agent finally had a clear target. He raised his .38 Special Charter Arms revolver in a two-hand grip and aimed at the shoulder blades of the closest goon.

Kalvo's hands trembled as he squeezed the trigger, causing his shots to travel higher than he'd intended. One bullet missed the gangster, but the other two smashed into the base of the hoodlum's skull.

When his comrade crumbled to the floor with a chunk of his head missing, Constantine Mercouri whirled and fired his Colt 1911A1 automatic at Kalvo. A .45 caliber slug slammed into the bridge of Paul Kalvo's nose. The back of his skull exploded. Yet a muscle reflex allowed Kalvo to fire his snub-nose revolver one last time.

Mercouri cried out and dropped his Colt. A .38 bullet had struck his shoulder, blasting cartilage that held the joint together. The gangster spun about to see the muzzle of the M-76 submachine gun aimed in his direction. Calvin James's face resembled an ebony carving of a Zulu war god as he calmly triggered his weapon.

Bullets crashed into Constantine Mercouri's chest. Blood splashed his brown leather jacket as the impact of multiple 9mm rounds kicked him back against the table. Man and furniture slammed to the floor in a lifeless, shattered heap.

"Calvin!" McCarter shouted when he saw a large figure bolt from the cover of the jukebox.

Strabo, the muscular limo driver, had scrambled to the shelter of the big music box when the shooting began. The big Greek did not carry a gun, so he simply stayed behind cover, kept his head low and waited.

But now, with all his companions dead, Strabo had only one chance to survive.

He attacked James with the only weapons he had—his hands and feet. James swung the M-76 at the chauffeur. Strabo's leg lashed out and a boot smacked into the S&W subgun. The kick struck the weapon from the antiterrorist's grasp.

McCarter aimed his Browning Hi-Power at Strabo's broad back but held his fire. James was too close to the Greek terrorist. McCarter was a superb pistol marksman. Yet he realized his wounded arm reduced his accuracy. Besides, a 9mm parabellum slug could punch clean through Strabo and hit James. McCarter cursed under his breath and hoped a better target would present itself.

Strabo followed his kick with a rapid *seiken* punch to the point of James's jaw. The black man's head bounced from the powerful karate blow. He staggered backward into the bar, his head lanced by shards of pain as bursts of light popped and blurred his vision.

Still, James saw the big Greek lunge forward. James dodged a vicious side kick that slammed into the panels of the bar. Wood cracked and the entire building seemed to tremble when Strabo's boot connected.

Strabo was good. He immediately slashed a cross-body *shuto* chop at James. The Phoenix Force warrior blocked the stroke with a forearm and swung a hook kick into the Greek's left kidney. Strabo bellowed in anger and pain. He used the bar for a brace and lashed a backward mule kick at his adversary.

James parried the kick with a karate chop to the

ankle. Strabo nearly lost his balance as he spun about to face the black warrior. James's right leg rocketed into a high crescent kick. The edge of his foot slammed into Strabo's cheekbone. The Greek's head spun from the force of the blow, but he did not fall.

Strong son of a bitch, James thought as he plowed a ram's-head punch to Strabo's solar plexus. The brute gasped, and James hooked his left fist into Strabo's jaw. The big bad dude still did not go down.

Strabo's left hand swung a "tiger claw" at James's face. The black man leaped away from the slashing fingers and launched a high roundhouse kick to the guy's head. James's boot crashed into the side of Strabo's skull, just above the vulnerable temple. The Greek's nervous system went out to lunch, and Strabo finally dropped senseless to the floor.

"Nice work, mate," McCarter remarked as he approached. His left hand clutched his bullet-torn upper arm.

"This dude was candy," James replied. He gingerly rubbed his sore chin. "Hardrock candy. Damn near broke my jaw. Let me take a look at your arm."

"It'll keep," McCarter told him. "Better cuff your sparring partner before he comes to. None of the rest of these jokers will be going anyplace until the meatwagon arrives."

"How about Kalvo?" James asked as he knelt to bind Strabo's wrists together behind his back with plastic riot cuffs.

"Caught a bullet right between the eyes." The battle-scarred McCarter sighed. "I had that bloke figured for a pantywaist, but he died like a real warrior."

"I know." The black man nodded. "Probably saved my life."

"Well, the Athens police will be here any minute," McCarter said. "We'd better contact Katz and Draco unless we want to wind up in a Greek jail tonight."

"Yeah," James agreed. "I think they're gonna be pissed when we tell them how this raid turned out."

"Why should they feel any different about it than us?" McCarter replied with a fatalistic shrug.

14

The window to Rafael Encizo's room was open. The Cuban explained that he had opened it earlier to test for alarms. Apparently the window would be safe to use as a method for sneaking out of the mansion.

"I also checked the sill for pressure plates," Encizo told Manning. "Some alarms are triggered by the weight of an intruder."

"How do you check for pressure plates?" the Canadian inquired, genuinely curious.

"The plates have to be made of metal," Encizo answered, "so I used a magnet. There aren't any plates here."

"What about sentries?" the Canadian asked.

"A pair of guards patrol outside," his partner said. "They just walk around the house in a circle. I timed them. Takes about fifteen minutes to make one round."

Manning stared out the window and gazed down the marble wall at the stone-paved ground two stories below. "What are we going to do?" he asked. "Hang a bed sheet outside and use it for a rope to shinny down to the ground?"

"We'd have to leave it dangling from the window," the Cuban answered. "That would be a dead giveaway to the sentries."

"So how are we going to get down there?"

Encizo replied by handing the Canadian his Sterling automatic. Then the Cuban climbed out the window. He gripped the sill with both hands and lowered his body over the edge. The Cuban gently swayed his dangling body like a pendulum. Then he let go.

He stayed close to the wall as he dropped. His foot hit the head jamb of a window on the first floor. Encizo seemed to bounce and whirl in midair. His feet hit the pavement. Encizo's bent knees allowed him to absorb the impact. Then he tumbled into a forward roll and smoothly sprang upright. Encizo looked up at Manning and smiled.

The Canadian whistled softly. "You gotta be kidding," he muttered under his breath.

Manning tossed the Sterling down to Encizo, then threw down his own Sterling and reluctantly climbed out the window. He seized the sill and dangled over the edge, trying to imitate his partner.

Encizo had made it look easy. Manning knew better. His heart seemed to throb in his windpipe as he hung on to the narrow ledge and swung his legs toward the window below. Manning clenched his teeth, hoped he would not break a leg and let go of the sill.

His foot hit the window jamb and slipped. Manning tried to pivot in the air. Pain shot through his left arm when his elbow struck the wall. The Canadian dropped to the ground. He landed feet first, but tumbled awkwardly when he tried to break his fall.

"Didn't break any bones, did you?" the Cuban inquired as he helped Manning rise.

"No," the Canadian replied, rubbing his sore arm. "But I sure got enough bruises."

"You didn't do badly for your first time," Encizo told him as he gave Manning his Sterling autoloader.

" 'First time'?" Manning glared at him. "You mean you've done that before?"

"This was my third time," the Cuban confirmed. "Of course, each drop is different because each building is designed differently. It's not always this easy."

"I'll take your word for it," Manning muttered. "I see your ankle has certainly healed."

Encizo winced slightly at the thought of the shot he took in the leg during a previous mission in Israel. He'd still been limping on the last assignment but was thankful he had recovered since. Encizo tapped Manning on the shoulder and the pair headed away from the mansion toward the opposite side of the island, where the terrorist camp had to be located.

"Do you have any brilliant ideas about how we'll get back through that window later?" Manning asked as they hurried from the house before the sentries could complete their rounds.

"Of course I do," Encizo replied. "But I don't think you want to hear about it."

"I don't think so, either," the Canadian admitted.

THEY FOUND THE BARRACKS SECTION easily enough with the help of the light from the moon. Two large billets-style buildings and a smaller structure made of concrete covered an area as big as two city blocks. Three sentries patroled the area. Each was armed with a Russian AK-47 assault rifle.

"What do you think, Gary?" Encizo asked as he and Manning crouched in the dense shadows under a tree a quarter of a mile from the barracks.

"I think we'll have to take out the guards," Manning replied grimly.

"That's what I think, too." The Cuban sighed. "That means we'll have to get off this island fast after we finish the recon mission. Any bright ideas about that? It's your turn to come up with some."

"We'll have to leave by boat." The Canadian shrugged. "Think you can handle Krio's yacht?"

"The *Argo*?" Encizo smiled. "Now that would be sailing away from here with style."

"First we have to finish our job," Manning remarked. "Now let's take care of those sentries."

GUARD DUTY MUST BE the dullest, most monotonous chore in the world, thought the sentry. Hours of walking around the same area in the same pattern, seeing the same buildings, the same shadows, hearing the same crickets chirping in the night, is boring.

The sentry paused and looked up at the sky. He was rehearsing what he would say to his wife when he told her he wanted a divorce. He muttered to himself and shook his head as he strolled to the corner of one of the billets. Suddenly his guts seemed to explode.

Gary Manning had lashed the side of his hand into the fellow's colon when he started to turn the corner. The guard doubled up with a groan. Manning quickly clasped his hands together and chopped them into the base of his opponent's neck. The vulnerable seventh vertebra cracked. Bone popped and the spinal cord snapped. The sentry fell. He was vaguely aware he was dying before the world seemed to be swallowed up in a black hole.

Another sentry heard his comrade's groan and

headed toward the sound. He passed right by Rafael Encizo, who was hidden among the shadows between the billets and the concrete structure. The Cuban pounced like *el tigre* and attacked the man from behind.

Encizo clamped a palm over the guard's mouth and promptly thrust the point of his Gerber into the man's left kidney. Sharp steel pierced the vital organ. The sentry convulsed violently. Encizo held him firmly and drew the knife across the man's throat. Blood vomited from the hideous wound. The Cuban felt his opponent's muscles relax. Only then did he allow the corpse to fall to the ground.

The third sentry saw Encizo kill his comrade. The man unslung his AK-47 and prepared to work the bolt. Manning rushed up behind the guard and quickly lashed out with the barrel of the rifle he had taken from the first guard. Steel crashed into the man's skull.

Dazed, the sentry fell to the ground. Manning kicked the Kalashnikov out of the man's grasp. The guard made a feeble grab for the Canadian's ankle. Manning's foot swung into the man's face, and the guard sprawled on his back with a groan. The Phoenix Force fighter stamped the edge of his shoe into the sentry's throat, crushing the thyroid cartilage. Blood bubbled from the man's open mouth.

Manning dragged the corpse into the shadows and searched him. The Canadian found two extra magazines for the AK-47 and a .45 Government Issue Colt automatic. Manning preferred large-caliber handguns. He did not trust anything that did not have enough stopping power to knock a man on his ass with one slug. The Canadian thrust the Colt into his belt and stuffed the spare magazines into his pockets.

"Gary," Encizo called softly as he approached. The Cuban also carried an AK-47 he'd confiscated from a dead sentry. "Nobody else is wandering around, but there are lights on in a couple of windows."

"Think anyone saw or heard us take out these guys?" Manning asked.

"Looks like we're okay for now," Encizo replied. "I just hope we don't have to do any shooting. I figure we'll be outnumbered about fifty to one if that happens."

"Yeah." Manning nodded. "I wish we had silencers for these weapons. Let's get to work before somebody decides to check on the guards and finds them lying down on the job."

The Phoenix Force pair moved to the concrete building. Since this was the only reinforced structure, they decided it must contain the most important materials. Encizo took one look at the door and cursed softly in Spanish.

It was made of steel and had no handle or keyhole. A push-button panel was installed beside the door. One would have to press a numeral code in sequence in order to activate the computer-programmed lock. An incorrect sequence would probably trigger an alarm.

"Can you crack it, Rafael," Manning whispered tensely.

"Not with just a set of lock picks," the Cuban replied. "Looks like we're—"

An electrical hum startled the pair, and the door

slowly swung open. Manning and Encizo quickly moved behind it. A lone figure dressed in a laboratory smock stepped outside. He inhaled deeply, sighed and reached into a pocket for a pack of cigarettes.

Gary Manning grabbed the man from behind and delivered a solid *seiken* punch to the mastoid bone behind his left ear. The man in white groaned softly and slumped unconscious into Manning's arms.

Rafael Encizo charged through the open doorway, AK-47 held ready. He nearly collided with a large beefy man who had drawn a pistol from the button-flap holster on his hip. The Cuban rapidly swung his Kalashnikov and chopped the barrel across the man's wrist. Bone snapped, and the pistol fell from the terrorist's fingers.

A backhand sweep rapped the AK-47 across the gunman's face. The blow knocked the guy against a wall. Encizo stabbed the muzzle of his rifle into his opponent's solar plexus. The terrorist doubled up, and Encizo brought the stock of his Kalashnikov down on the base of the goon's skull. He dropped like a sack of shit at Encizo's feet.

Manning hauled the man in white across the threshold. He glanced about the room. It seemed to be a foyer, with a field desk facing the door. Apparently this was a guard station for the man Encizo had knocked unconscious.

"Rafael," Manning whispered, pointing at a trio of television monitors mounted on the wall above the desk.

"I see them," the Cuban replied. "They've got a goddamn closed-circuit television surveillance system."

"But we didn't find any cameras outside," the Canadian remarked.

"They must be out there somewhere," Encizo said. "Or why would they have this TV system? We're in a hell of a lot of trouble, amigo."

The door suddenly swung shut like the lid to a steel coffin. It locked automatically. The two Phoenix Force commandos felt as if they had just been sealed inside a tomb.

15

Rafael Encizo stepped toward the TV monitors and examined the screens. The Cuban sighed with relief when he discovered the surveillance system was not connected to cameras posted outside the building. Images of three emaciated men in separate rooms were being transmitted to the television receivers.

"The closed-circuit system isn't to watch for intruders," Encizo remarked. "It's to spy on prisoners."

"Yeah," Manning agreed. "Looks like they've got those poor devils locked in padded cells. The kind used in mental institutions to confine violent psychos. Wonder who those guys are?"

"Let's find out," the Cuban suggested as he moved to the man in the white lab coat.

Encizo rubbed the carotid artery in the guy's neck. The Cuban had once seen Keio Ohara use this technique to revive an unconscious person by stimulating the flow of blood to the brain. The man groaned weakly.

Still imitating Ohara, Encizo grabbed the guy's hand and applied pressure to his fingernails. Unfamiliar with the finer points of the Japanese art of *atemi*, Encizo could not recall the second part of the technique.

He decided to use the Occidental method, instead. Encizo slapped the man's face and shook him hard. *"¡Qué la chigada!"* the Cuban snapped. "Wake up, you bastard."

The man's eyes popped open. He saw the muzzle of a Sterling M-302 aimed at his face. Encizo thumbed off the safety.

"You want to die?" Encizo asked in his clumsy Greek.

"Yah n'ye ponimahyu," the captive rasped fearfully. *"Vee guvaritey po-rooski?"*

"Cristo," Encizo muttered. "This guy isn't Greek. He's a goddamn Russian."

"'Russian'?" Manning frowned. "Well, you speak Russian, don't you?"

"Not fluently," the Cuban admitted. "My Russian isn't much better than my Greek. Sure wish Yakov were here."

"You're the best we've got right now," the Canadian told him.

"Okay," Encizo turned to the Russian. *"Kak vas zavoot?"*

"My name is Chekov," the man answered. "Dr. Chekov."

"'Doctor'?" Encizo narrowed his eyes. "Did the KGB send you to help produce the starvation substance?"

Chekov knitted his bushy eyebrows. Encizo had mispronounced several words in Russian and he had constructed the sentence incorrectly. Chekov was not certain he understood the Cuban.

"You refer to the Proteus Enzyme, yes?" the Russian inquired.

" 'Proteus Enzyme'?" Encizo raised an eyebrow. "That's what you call it. Yes, Citizen Doctor. We know about your project here, but we want to know more."

"I am not a biochemist," Chekov explained. "Dr. Petrov can tell you how the enzyme is produced. That is not my field."

"What is your field?" the Cuban asked. "What is your job here?"

"I am a nutritional consultant," the Russian replied proudly. "Once I served as an official dietitian to the cosmonauts."

"Impressive credentials for a prison doctor," Encizo remarked, jerking his head toward the TV screens. "Those men are your patients, yes?"

"They are subjects for experiment and research," Chekov answered stiffly.

"Human guinea pigs," Encizo remarked in English. He switched back to Russian. "Where are these 'subjects' being held?"

"The cells are located in this building," the Russian answered. "I'll take you there."

"Are there any more guards or doctors like you lurking around here?"

"No," Chekov assured him. "The guard stationed here and I are the only persons on duty in this building."

"No tricks, Doctor," the Cuban warned. "I know the propaganda campaigns in the Kremlin try to convince all the Soviet people that Americans are murderous gangsters. It is not true, Doctor. We won't kill you unless you fail to cooperate."

"Would you admit it if you intended to kill me?" Chekov asked dryly.

"Probably not," Encizo confessed. "But I wouldn't promise to spare your life unless I intended to do so."

"There is another guard stationed at the cell block." Chekov sighed.

"Continue to cooperate and you'll stay alive, Doctor," Encizo told him.

Manning had bound and gagged the unconscious sentry. Encizo explained his conversation with Chekov to the Canadian. Manning cast a suspicious glance at the Russian. "You think we can trust him?" he asked.

"I don't think he's KGB," Encizo replied. "I wouldn't go so far as to say we can trust him, but I don't think he's lying. Frankly, he's the only guide we've got."

"Great," the Canadian muttered. "Well, I guess we don't have much choice."

Encizo turned to Chekov and nodded. The Russian led the Phoenix Force pair to another door. Manning and his Cuban partner stiffened when Chekov reached for a panel of buttons identical to the one at the front entrance. The Soviet doctor pressed several buttons.

No alarms betrayed them. The door opened with an electrical hum. A man, seated at another field desk, gazed up at the trio. His eyes expanded with shock when he saw the two armed strangers with Chekov. The guard reached for a pistol on his hip.

"Nyet, Illya!" Chekov cried. *"Nyet!"*

The sentry ignored him and drew his pistol. Encizo's Sterling M-302 cracked twice. A pair of tiny holes appeared in Illya's forehead. Twin streams of blood squirted from the exit wounds at the back of his skull. The sentry collapsed across his desk.

"I had no choice, Doctor," the Cuban told Chekov.

"I know," the Russian replied sadly.

"Where are the prisoners?" Encizo asked.

Chekov led the Phoenix Force commandos to a corridor. The Russian moved to yet another wall panel and pressed several buttons. Three doors slid open in response.

Manning advanced first, his AK-47 held ready. He cautiously peered into the first room. A skeletal figure lay on a cot. He barely raised his head to look at Manning.

The Canadian moved to the next cell. Another emaciated figure sat on a cot. He wearily turned his head to face Manning. His cheeks were hollow and his eyes were as expressionless as the glass orbs of a mannequin.

The man in the third cell was too weak even to raise his head. His diaphragm rose and fell slightly.

Manning heard the soft wheeze of labored breathing. The Canadian's face was hard with anger when he turned to Encizo and Chekov. "Ask the 'doctor' if he's proud of his work," he said angrily.

The Cuban nudged Chekov with his Kalashnikov and ushered him into the corridor. Encizo's stomach knotted with the same kind of anger and revulsion expressed by Manning. "Why are you doing this?" the Cuban asked Chekov. "How can you justify this kind of research?"

"Previous experiments were conducted in Siberia," Chekov replied. "But we had to be certain the

Proteus Enzyme would work in a warm climate on healthy subjects.''

" 'Subjects'?'' Encizo spat. "You mean, *victims*.''

"Yes.'' The Russian nodded. "I agree it is horrible. These men are innocent victims of a war between your government and mine. I do not understand politics. *Pravda* prints lies. Moscow distorts truth. Yet is this not true of Washington, as well? I simply follow orders. The same as you, yes?''

"No,'' the Cuban told him. "I wouldn't obey an order to kill innocent people. I wouldn't agree to conduct experiments such as these.''

"Rafael,'' Manning began. "We're running out of time. Better ask Doc Ivan where the laboratory is.''

"What do we do then?'' Encizo asked. "Destroy it?''

"Why not?'' The Canadian shrugged. "I've got enough C-4 in my belt to blow up half this building.''

"And what if the Proteus Enzyme is carried by the wind, or multiplies when exposed to oxygen or light?'' the Cuban inquired. "They sure as hell don't have such tight security just to hold three half-dead prisoners in their cells. Who can say how fast the virus might spread if it leaks out of here.''

"I'll just use enough explosives to destroy the lab,'' the demolitions expert assured him. "Then we'll seal this place up. We'd better take a sample of the enzyme with us for our scientists to analyze.''

"Voitha'o," a voice called weakly from one of the cells. *"Parakalo, voitha'o...."*

"He's begging for help,'' Encizo told Manning.

"They're too sick to travel,'' the Canadian stated

grimly. "I hate the idea of leaving them here, but I don't see how we can help them."

"Madre de Dios," Encizo whispered. "I hate this mission."

Without warning, an orange mist spewed from air vents in the ceiling. It poured into the cells and through the corridor. A strong, sickly sweet scent similar to almond extract assaulted their nostrils. The Phoenix Force pair realized instantly what the strange odor meant—cyanide gas.

Manning and Encizo bolted from the corridor. Chekov followed. They dashed past the corpse of Illya and fled to the foyer.

The door to the front entrance stood open. Half a dozen figures waited at the threshold. Some were shirtless, clad only in fatigue trousers, but all wore gas masks and carried rifles. Three men had adopted a kneeling stance, while the others stood. All six aimed their weapons at the Phoenix Force duo.

The gunmen did not give Encizo and Manning a chance either to defend themselves or surrender. The terrorist troops immediately triggered their rifles. Bullets crashed into Manning's upper torso. The impact hurled him backward into a wall. Stunned by the throbbing pain in his chest, Manning slid to the floor. He saw Encizo double up and fall beside him.

The Canadian tried to raise his AK-47. A figure stepped forward and stamped a boot on the rifle to pin it to the floor.

The terrorist leaned forward and aimed a Russian Makarov pistol at Manning's head. "Bang, bang, American," he announced in broken English distorted by the filters of his gas mask. "You're dead."

16

"This is a disaster!" Andrew McCullum said angrily. "Two full-scale gun battles in the streets of Athens. More than a dozen men killed—including one of my people."

Yakov Katzenelenbogen quietly sat in a wicker chair in the front room of the operations' safehouse. He did not interrupt McCullum. The Israeli could not blame the guy for being upset. Katz was not terribly happy about the results of the mission thus far, either.

Officially Andrew McCullum was a member of diplomatic corps for the United States embassy in Athens. In reality he was the control officer for CIA operations in Greece. Paul Kalvo had been one of his field agents.

"Mr. McCullum," Manos Draco began. "I was with Mr. Goldblum when our car was attacked. We really had no choice."

"He shouldn't have insisted on playing idiot games with those gangsters in the first place," McCullum responded. "What could you possibly hope to gain?"

"It was a lead," Katz replied. "The only one we could pursue in Athens."

"And what have you and your overzealous companions accomplished?'' McCullum persisted. ''We're no closer to proving Krio's role in a Communist conspiracy than we were before. I don't mind telling you, Goldblum, there's going to be an investigation of you and your people. We'll find out how you lunatics managed to get your authority. The White House will cut you off. You'll never screw up another Company operation like this. . . .''

''The mission isn't over yet,'' Katz remarked, removing a cigarette from a pack of Camels.

''As far as you and your kill-happy friends are concerned it is,'' the CIA control stated.

''You don't have the authority to pull us from the mission,'' the Israeli told him as he fired the cigarette with his battered Ronson. ''We're still in command, McCullum. Whether you like it or not.''

''Now see here, Goldblum,'' McCullum began.

''I've listened to you,'' Katz said forcefully. ''Now you can listen to me. Paul Kalvo was killed and one of my men was wounded tonight. Those are the only casualties on our side thus far. But two of my people are on Krio Island right now. I'm concerned about their safety, and I'm not about to pull out and abandon them.''

''That was another stupid mistake—''

''Let me finish,'' the Phoenix Force commander said sternly. ''We've got a job to do and we intend to finish it. I realize you try to conduct CIA operations quietly. The only way an intelligence network can be effective is by maintaining a low profile. I appreciate your position, McCullum. I understand your problems far better than I am at liberty to explain to you. But what's happening on Krio Island is too important to risk the success of our mission for the sake of the Company's public relations in Greece.''

"We've managed to keep a lid on everything so far," Draco added. "The media was told that both gun battles involved local gangsters and undercover police officers. Officially it's over now. The criminals are either dead or under arrest."

"Weren't all the crooks killed?" McCullum inquired.

"A man named Strabo was taken prisoner," Katz answered. "He's currently being held in a hospital under police guard."

"He's wounded?" the control officer asked.

"No," Yakov explained. "He's being questioned by Mr. Johnson."

"Johnson is the black guy, right?" McCullum frowned. "What sort of 'questioning' is he putting Strabo through?"

"Scopolamine," Katz said bluntly.

"What?" McCullum glared at him. "You can't have a man pumped full of truth serum in a goddamn public hospital."

"Tight security of the room is being maintained," the Israeli assured him. "No one goes in or out except Mr. Johnson."

"Who the hell is this Johnson?" the CIA man demanded. "Does he know what he's doing with scopolamine? That stuff can be fatal if it's misused."

"Johnson is aware of that," Katz declared. "He's qualified in the use of both medicine and chemicals. Besides, any risk to Strabo's life is justified under the circumstances. If he dies we'll simply tell the press he expired from injuries suffered during the gun battle."

"Christ," McCullum muttered. "You're a cold-blooded son of a bitch, Goldblum."

"Not as cold-blooded as the terrorists we're trying to stop," Katz replied. "Frankly, I'm more concerned about a threat to the lives of thousands of innocent people than I am about a single criminal henchman."

"That sounds like a car just pulled into the driveway," Draco remarked when he heard gravel crunch beneath tires. "I hope it's Nikkos and Miller."

The Greek intel agent moved to a window and peered outside. Then he unlocked the front door and opened it. Nikkos Papadopoulos entered, followed by David McCarter. The Briton's right arm was in a sling, but he held his Browning Hi-Power in his left fist. A third figure stumbled across the threshold, propelled by a shove from Calvin James. The black man entered last and closed the door.

"Anyway," McCarter told Nikkos, "this bloody Scot was as drunk as a lord, so he didn't even realize he'd torn his ruddy kilt...."

"What's going on?" McCullum demanded.

"Who's this bloke?" McCarter asked, shoving the Browning into his belt.

"A confused man who deserves some explanations," Katz replied. He approached the unwilling visitor, whom James had pushed into the room. "Mr. Xerxes, I presume?"

"In the flesh," James confirmed as he opened his Windbreaker to return a Colt Commander to shoulder leather. "This is Theo Xerxes, top dog of the Athens criminal garbage heap. Picked him up at his home half an hour ago, and he's been crying for a lawyer ever since."

"I didn't hear him say nothin' like that." Nikkos grinned. "'Course, Miller and me was chattin' a bit 'bout Jolly Ol' England and what not."

"Did you know Nikkos used to live in Great Britain?" McCarter inquired. "That's where he learned to speak English."

"I never would have guessed," Katz said dryly.

"You know what it was like being in the same car with these two," James remarked. "I felt like I was inside a British pub on wheels."

"Wait a minute," McCullum insisted. "You mean you kidnapped this man and brought him here?"

"We had to kidnap the bastard." McCarter shrugged. "Don't have enough evidence to arrest him."

"I will not be party to an illegal abduction," the CIA man declared.

"You're already party to it," Katz told him. "And you may get to witness a lot worse unless Xerxes cooperates with us."

"I demand to make a telephone call," Xerxes announced in surprisingly good English. "You people are making a serious mistake."

Without warning, Katzenelenbogen smacked the back of his left hand across the gangster's face. Xerxes stumbled backward into Calvin James, who abruptly shoved him into a chair.

"You're not in a position to demand anything, Xerxes," Katz snapped. "You're not getting anything unless we decide to let you have it. No lawyer. No phone call. You won't even get your next breath if we decide to deny you of it."

"Told you we weren't working for the Peace Corps," James said to Xerxes.

"I can't condone this sort of behavior..." Mc-Cullum began.

"We're not interested in your bloody approval," McCarter informed him. "We're going to get some answers from this bastard. Whatever it takes to make him talk. If we have to turn this room into a bleedin' torture chamber, we'll damn well do it."

McCullum's mouth fell open in mute horror. Xerxes stiffened. Manos Draco and Nikkos stared at the Phoenix Force trio, uncertain if the commandos would actually resort to torture.

But Katz, McCarter and James all knew that Phoenix Force had been created to combat brutality, not participate in it. They had no intention of carrying out McCarter's threat. Not only did they find torture repulsive, they also realized it was a time-consuming, frequently unreliable method.

"Mr. Johnson," Katz began. "Did you learn anything from Strabo?"

"Gave me a full confession," James replied. "Told me quite a few details about Xerxes here. That's how we found him. Strabo knew what rock to look under. Also confirmed that Krio is the real boss of the syndicate. Mr. X is just his lieutenant."

"Did you get all this on tape?" the Israeli inquired.

"Naturally," James said as he took a Memorex cassette from a pocket. "Among other things, Strabo mentioned that he works as a limo driver for Krio. Guess who he picked up at the airport today? Anthony Peters and Ramón Santos."

Katz instantly recognized the cover names being used by Manning and Encizo. "Is Krio suspicious of them?"

"Seems to figure there's a fifty-fifty chance they're spies." The black man nodded. "At least that was the impression Strabo got. The guy doesn't know anything about the Bulgarians except they've got something big going on on the island. Strabo figured it was some sort of arms-smuggling operation."

"That tape won't be admissable in court," McCullum said curtly. "You've got the confession and other information by illegal means."

"Whose bloody side are you on, you arse?" McCarter said angrily. "Trying to help Xerxes?"

"Don't be upset, Mr. McCullum," Katz urged. "Xerxes isn't going to stand trial."

The Greek gangster glared at Katz. "What is that suppose to mean?"

"You have a choice, Xerxes," the Israeli told him, crushing out his cigarette in an ashtray. "You're going to tell us everything you know about Krio and his connection with the Bulgarians."

"I don't know what you're talking about." Xerxes shrugged.

"Reconsider that answer," Katz warned. "We're prepared to offer you a deal, Xerxes. I don't like making deals with scum like you. It's offensive. But sometimes we have to do things we don't like in this business."

"What kind of deal?" the hoodlum asked tensely.

"You tell us about Krio's operations," Katz began. "His ties to the syndicate, the Bulgarians, everything."

"We want you to make like a canary," James added. "Spill your guts. Squeal your head off. Do a Joe Valachi. Get the picture?"

"What happens if I talk?" Xerxes wanted to know.

"You'll be transported to another country and given a new identity," Katz explained. "You'll receive protection. No one can promise the KGB won't track you down. Their Morkrie Delia assassination section is very good. But how long do you think you'll last without our help?"

"And if I don't cooperate?" the gangster asked.

"Then Mr. Miller and Mr. Johnson will extract a confession from you, anyway." Katz sighed. "But it will be very unpleasant for you, Xerxes."

"Not for me." McCarter chuckled as he lit a Player's cigarette. "I'd love to work on this bloke. Ever have your eyeballs used for an ashtray, Xerxes?"

"Miller's methods are crude," James said, continuing the charade. "But they generally get results. Of course, you're a tough guy, so you probably won't break after just a couple hours of torture. That's when I'll give you a dose of scopolamine."

"After you've been tortured and injected with truth serum," Draco began, playing along with Phoenix Force. "We can't let you live."

"You're bluffing," Xerxes said, but his voice trembled. "If you're serious, you'd simply start working me over. Why offer to deal, instead?"

"Because you might die before you get around to talking," Katz answered. "Heart failure, shock, too much stress on the spinal cord—all are common when torture is employed."

"Scopolamine is risky, too," James added. "I had Strabo hooked up to a polygraph at the hospital so I could watch his heartbeat, blood pressure and all that. No way I can do that here. Your goddamn heart might explode like a water-filled balloon dropped from a fourth-story window."

"The choice is simple, Xerxes," Katz told him. "Life or death."

"I'll deal," the gangster declared grimly.

"Goldblum," McCullum said sharply. "I want to talk to you. Privately, if you don't mind."

Katz and the CIA control officer moved to the kitchen. McCullum thrust an accusing finger at the Israeli. He was so angry his body trembled as if he suffered from malaria.

"You don't have a right to bargain with that man," McCullum declared.

"Does Krio have a right to operate criminal and terrorist activities in Greece?" Katz replied sternly. "Does the KGB have a right to develop a malnutrition virus to use on innocent people?"

"That's not the issue," McCullum snapped.

"Yes, it is," Katz insisted. "If corruption wasn't ignored because men like Krio have powerful friends, we wouldn't be faced with this situation. If the governments and the public in general would recognize the fact that the KGB is more than just an intelligence network for the Soviet Union, we wouldn't be forced to use such desperate methods now. The Komitet Gosudarstvennoi Bezopasnosti is an international evil that manipulates, schemes and murders to try to destroy freedom throughout the world."

"I'm CIA," McCullum stated. "Why lecture me about this?"

"Because you're a bureaucrat," the Israeli told him. "The CIA has become too concerned with public opinion. The Company can't keep secrets, it can seldom act effectively and it's oversensitive to criticism when it does. You're not accustomed to confronting the dragon and fighting it tooth and claw. That, my friend, is exactly what we must do before this nightmare will be over.''

Before McCullum could respond, Calvin James entered the kitchen. ''Xerxes is blabbing his head off into a tape recorder,'' James began. ''He says they're conducting human experiments on the island to test something called the Proteus Enzyme. And you know our friends haven't returned from Krio Island yet.''

''I realize that.'' The Israeli nodded. ''But their safety isn't as important as stopping Krio and the terrorists.''

''Yeah,'' James agreed. ''And that's something we'd better do damn fast. Xerxes claims they'll start shipping out the terrorists tomorrow morning.''

''Draco once mentioned he can get assistance from the Greek parachute regiment,'' Katz commented. ''Said there's an entire battalion on standby. Looks like it's time to call them in.''

''But you claimed an air strike was an unacceptable solution,'' McCullum said.

''We can't let the terrorists off that island,'' Katz replied. ''We're running out of time, and we only have one choice of action left.''

''Miller isn't in any shape to go into combat,'' James commented. ''His wound isn't really serious, but there is some damage to muscle tissue that needs to heal first. Better order him not to go on the raid.''

'' 'Order him not to go'?'' Katz rolled his eyes,

familiar with McCarter's addiction to action. "We'll probably have to knock him out and lock him in an iron lung to keep him from coming with us."

"You people can't simply launch a raid on Krio Island," McCullum stated in a stunned voice.

"We can," Katz corrected. "And we will. Because it's the only chance we've got to prevent an international massacre from taking place."

17

Gary Manning and Rafael Encizo were unceremoniously dragged outside. The terrorists dumped them facedown on the ground. Hands quickly searched the pair and confiscated their weapons.

Manning glanced up to find himself surrounded by a forest of legs with booted feet. The Canadian's arms were twisted behind his back. He heard steel click and felt the pinch of handcuffs as they locked around his wrists.

"Good evening, gentlemen," a voice declared.

Two terrorists hauled Manning to his feet. The barrel-chested explosives expert blinked and shook his head to clear his blurred vision. He recognized the face that materialized before him.

Colonel Nikolai Kostov bowed curtly. "I can see that you recognize me, American," Kostov declared. "I've tried to keep a low profile, but no one can remain invisible forever. Since you know me, what shall I call you?" Manning was busy gasping air into his lungs. His chest ached. Yet he did not feel the awful gouged sensation that accompanies a bullet wound. He glanced down at his shirt. It was not stained with blood.

"Oh." Kostov laughed. "You're wondering why you aren't dead, eh? After all, you were shot point-blank in the chest. We wanted you alive, so we used rubber bullets.''

'' 'Rubber'?'' Manning rasped.

"Yes," the Bulgarian confirmed. "Rubber bullets were once used as a nonlethal form of riot control back in the sixties. They're still employed by the British in Northern Ireland. We have a supply for certain training exercises. You're a bit bruised, but you aren't really hurt."

"Gary?" Encizo's voice called hoarsely. "You okay, amigo?"

The battered Canadian turned his head toward his partner. Encizo stood between a brace of terrorist goons. The Cuban's hands had also been cuffed behind his back. Manning nodded to assure his partner that he was not injured.

"I'm so glad you're both able to speak," Kostov remarked. "I've got a few questions for you two. I'm going to order Captain Vitosho to escort you to the officers' quarters."

Kostov gestured at the armed figures who surrounded the Phoenix Force pair. Perhaps a dozen wore gas masks. The rest were clad in a variety of garments. Many were barefoot or dressed only in trousers or undershorts. One young female killer displayed her firm round breasts as she stood naked except for a pair of lace panties.

Some terrorists were armed with assault rifles. Others held submachine guns or pistols. They glared at the captives. Their eyes burned with the sadistic bloodlust that is common to terrorists regardless of sex, nationality or political ideology.

Despite all their claims of devotion to a "righteous

cause for the sake of mankind,'' destruction is the great passion that motivates a terrorist. Their vicious breed craves devastation and murder the way a vampire thirsts for blood, Manning thought as he surveyed the scum.

''These comrades of the people's liberation,'' Kostov began, unable to keep a snicker from his tone, ''are very upset because you killed several of their blood brothers tonight. They'd like nothing better than to tear you limb from limb like an insect in the hands of a cruel child. I suggest you don't try to resist. Captain Vitosho is really much more civilized than the rest of this crowd.''

A tall, muscular blond man stripped off his gas mask and smiled at Encizo and Manning. They recognized Captain Igor Vitosho, the Bulgarian paratrooper and commando. Vitosho gestured with his Makarov to indicate one of the billets.

''Try to run, I shoot you in leg,'' Vitosho warned. ''Move. Now, please.''

''Who can resist such flawless manners?'' Encizo muttered sourly as he shuffled toward the building.

Vitosho and two armed goons escorted Manning and Encizo to the officers' quarters. The interior surprised the Phoenix Force warriors. They entered a quaint room with a sofa, armchairs and an old-fashioned rolltop desk.

''Sit,'' Vitosho commanded. ''Chairs, please.''

''What's this room?'' Manning inquired as he lowered himself into one of the armchairs. ''The officers' lounge?''

''Is room for officers of people's republic to rest and reflect on their duties to country and to war for worldwide socialism," Vitosho replied as if reciting a religious creed.

"Then I was right." The Canadian shrugged. "It's the officers' lounge."

Kostov entered a few seconds later. He approached the pair and folded his arms on his chest. The Bulgarian colonel shook his head sadly.

"I told Krio not to let you come to the island," he declared. "It was another stupid mistake that Greek made. He's made several already."

"Well, he's an amateur," Manning commented. "It must gripe a professional like you to have to work with a guy like Krio."

"He's a very shrewd man," Kostov began as he took a gunmetal cigarette case from his pocket. "But basically a greedy capitalist, better suited to the cutthroat world of international trade than the shadowy domain of espionage. Greed and arrogance are his weaknesses."

"What's your main vice, Kostov?" Encizo enquired. "Power? Murder? Genocide?"

"I am following orders," the Bulgarian answered as he lit a Russian black cigarette. "I did not ask for this assignment. Frankly, I do not like it. But that is a moot point, since all of us must obey our superiors."

"Maybe guys like you ought to start refusing orders," Encizo suggested. "Or do something about the bastards who issue them."

"That's a naive remark for a professional to make," Kostov said. "And you're both obviously professionals."

"We can't be too good, or we wouldn't have been

captured.'' Manning sighed. "What did we do wrong?''

"Just a stroke of bad luck,'' the Bulgarian explained. "Captain Vitosho decided to check on the guards. When he found them dead, he alerted the rest of us. Then we saw you on our television monitors.''

"Shit,'' Encizo grunted. "It figures the closed-circuit system would be transmitting to more than one set of monitors. I should have guessed that.''

"Your security setup is very imaginative, Colonel,'' the Canadian remarked. "That false cyanide gas was a clever trick.''

" 'False'?'' Kostov raised his eyebrows. "Why do you think the cyanide wasn't genuine?''

"You wouldn't have used poison gas if you wanted us alive,'' Manning answered. "Besides, even brief exposure to cyanide gas would have made us pretty sick. Also, your troops with the rubber bullets wore gas masks, but some of them didn't wear shirts, and none of them had gloves or headgear. They would have needed better protection, since cyanide gas seeps through the pores of skin, as well as into nostrils and mouths.''

"Very good.'' The Bulgarian smiled. "It was actually a rather mild tear-gas compound with an almond scent. However, if it had been necessary, there is a secondary gas-tank linkup that would have ejected genuine cyanide into the corridors.''

"Naturally,'' Encizo sneered. "You wouldn't have been concerned about Dr. Chekov or the three human subjects you tested the Proteus Enzyme on.''

"How much do you know about the Proteus Enzyme?'' Kostov demanded.

"We're not really your problem now," Encizo said, twisting about in his chair as if trying to get in a more comfortable position. "You ought to be more concerned about our friends who have already prepared to stop your terrorist flunkies from slipping out of here to spread the enzyme to other countries."

Kostov stared at Encizo and Manning, trying to read their expressions and body language. The men of Phoenix Force had been trained to conceal physical signs of stress. Kostov frowned and drew deeply on his cigarette.

"Your friends can't know very much, or they wouldn't have sent you here," the Bulgarian said. "You probably guessed about the plans to use the terrorists—as you call them—as sabotage agents."

"Are we guessing that the enzyme was developed in the Soviet Union?" Manning added. "Or that it's been tested on prisoners in Siberian labor camps?"

"Chekov could have told you that." Kostov shrugged.

"One of the victims was Uri Yosefthal." The Canadian smiled. "He was sent to the United States, where he died of malnutrition. Our scientists have already put together the formula for Proteus and our intel people know the KGB is responsible."

"That's impossible," Kostov stated. "If you're really familiar with the Proteus Enzyme, tell me about the frog."

Neither Manning nor Encizo could think of a bluff concerning a frog. The Bulgarian smiled.

"There is a small species of tree frog native to Australia that has such a ridiculously long Latin name only a zoologist would bother to memorize it,"

Kostov explained. "However, this frog has a single unique ability found nowhere else in the animal kingdom. The female swallows her eggs and actually gives birth to her young *inside her stomach*."

Kostov smashed the tip of his cigarette into a brass ashtray. "Scientists around the world have been interested in this strange little frog for that reason. They've been trying to determine why the frog doesn't digest its young. If they can unravel this secret, it may lead to new methods for treating ulcers, digestive problems, even stomach cancer."

"Or the Proteus Enzyme," Manning remarked grimly.

"That is already a reality," Kostov said. "Last year, a Russian scientist doing research on the tree frog discovered the Proteus formula quite by accident. The chemical enzyme he developed is similar to the natural process of the tree frog that prevents it from digesting its young. I'm not a chemist and I don't claim to understand how such things work, but the enzyme causes a chain reaction in warm-blooded animals. Man, of course, is a mammal, so this applies to him, as well.

"This chain reaction affects not only the stomach," Kostov continued. "All systems connected with digestion are altered. Even the blood doesn't carry nutrients to the rest of the body. This mutation is so dramatic that the enzyme was named Proteus, after the Greek sea god who could transform himself into any creature or object."

"And the KGB naturally saw this as a wonderful addition to their chemical-warfare arsenal," Manning said with disgust.

"Biochemical warfare is a loathsome business," Kostov agreed. "But is nuclear war more acceptable?"

"Nobody has launched missiles at Mother Russia," Encizo declared.

"Only because the USSR can fire back with her own nuclear weapons," Kostov insisted. "Eventually one of the superpowers—it does not matter who starts it—will trigger a terrible war of devastation that will annihilate civilization as we know it."

"And you think the Proteus Enzyme is a better solution?" Encizo asked. "That's insane, Kostov. How can you defend the use of a weapon like that? You're an intelligent, rational man. How can you condone a chemical that will cause thousands of innocent people to die of malnutrition?"

"Thousands are dying of malnutrition in Third World countries." The Bulgarian shrugged. "Are their lives less important than those of Americans?"

"That's bullshit and you know it," Manning said bluntly. "People in underdeveloped countries aren't suffering because somebody infected them with a man-made enzyme for the purpose of conquest. Your comparison isn't valid, Kostov. So no more cheap shots unless you've got one that isn't stupid."

"Do you like this comparison better?" Kostov began. "Thousands will die from the Proteus Enzyme, true. Yet millions, if not *billions*, will be killed in a nuclear war."

"That's your idea of a better excuse?" Encizo scoffed, once again squirming in his chair. "That makes as much sense as committing suicide because you *might* get cancer in the future."

The door suddenly flung open, and Dimitri Krio angrily stomped into the room. Kostov smiled, obviously pleased by the tycoon's reaction.

"Your houseguests were restless, comrade," the Bulgarian told him. "We found them poking about the lab building. They've really been rather naughty...."

"Aren't you getting tired of gloating, Colonel?" Krio inquired stiffly.

"They killed four men..." Kostov began.

"Damn it!" the Greek snapped. "It's pointless to lecture me. All I can tell you is that my people searched their luggage and clothing. They found nothing suspicious. The guards who patrolled outside the house reported nothing unusual."

"Which proves your people are as incompetent as you are, Krio," Kostov stated.

"We can trade insults later," Krio growled. "I want to know why the tanks are being moved."

"I ordered the troops to transport the canisters to the boats," Kostov replied curtly. "We can't afford to wait until tomorrow."

"Tanks?" Encizo inquired.

"That's right," Kostov answered. "You two didn't see the tanks. You only got to the cell block. The laboratory is located at a lower level. A storage section is also underground. Tanks containing the Proteus Enzyme are kept there."

"That explains the tight security of that building," Encizo remarked. "Proteus must be pretty unstable."

"'Unstable'?" Krio laughed. "Don't you mean deadly?"

The Greek turned to the open door and snapped an order at one of the men outside. A bearded terrorist entered, carrying a diver's air tank by its harness straps. Krio abruptly took the canister and hauled it into the room.

"Be careful with that," Kostov warned.

"This tank contains enough enzyme to infect a small city," the Greek declared, his eyes burning fiercely. "Proteus is in a gaseous form. Released into the air, it can be spread by the wind over a ten-mile radius without its losing any of its lethal potential.

"The tanks are disguised as scuba gear so they can be smuggled on the boats without attracting suspicion," Kostov added. "The agents will be transported with the tanks to target areas in West Germany, Japan, Great Britain, Canada and, of course, the United States."

"How will they use the gas?" Manning inquired. "By flying over a city and spraying it like crop-dusting?"

"Nothing so obvious," the Bulgarian colonel replied. "A tank need only be placed on a rooftop and exploded by a simple time bomb. Virtually all terrorists know how to use such a device. The wind will do the rest."

"You guys are cannon fodder," Manning declared. "You're being used by the KGB because they realize this is too risky to succeed. You may kill a lot of people, but the scheme will be discovered before you can begin to actually weaken an entire nation."

"The KGB supports terrorists because they cause unrest, fear and distrust in other countries," Encizo added. "Terrorists aren't expected to topple governments. They're suppose to upset the population and contribute to turmoil. You're dreaming if you think you'll accomplish more than that with this Proteus Enzyme crap.''

''You both seem to forget that the effects of the enzyme are not immediate,'' Krio stated. ''How much alarm will a few hundred or even a thousand minor explosions on rooftops cause? Remember, these will occur all over the world. Tiny little incidents that appear to harm no one. Individually, they will hardly merit mention in a local newspaper. No one will become ill until a few days later. By the time anyone connects the explosions with the rash of bizarre deaths that follow, it will be too late.''

''What do you have to gain from this, Krio?'' Encizo demanded. ''What did the KGB offer a millionaire to make him participate in such lunacy?''

''The Soviet Union is going to become the ruling force throughout the world,'' the Greek answered. ''When that happens, I will become the supreme commander of all shipping trade in the Mediterranean. I'll also receive a position on the board of political affairs in Greece when the Soviets set up a new government here.''

Krio smiled when he saw the startled expressions on the faces of the Phoenix Force vets.

''It surprises you that I value a position of authority more than wealth?'' he asked. ''Money loses its value when you have more of it than you can possibly spend. You yearn for the things it cannot buy. My dear departed father cared only about money. He built his fortune and kept it by kowtowing to whoever was in charge of the government at the time. He groveled for the monarchs, and he licked the jack-boots of the Nazis. Whatever the rulers required, he gave it to them just to avoid harassment. Despite his wealth, he danced to their music.''

"And you'd rather dance to the Red Square Waltz?" Encizo sneered.

"I will be one of the most powerful men in the world," the Greek stated. "For that, I would happily make a deal with Satan himself."

"You're assuming this plan will succeed," Manning said, "and that the KGB will honor their promises. Do you honestly think you can trust them? If so, you obviously don't know what kind of people you're dealing with."

"That is my concern," Krio said as he placed the gas canister on the floor. "But you won't live to know the outcome."

He removed a small, slender metal tube from his shirt pocket. It resembled a miniature spray can of chemical mace. The Greek aimed it at Gary Manning's face.

"This is a little contraption that's already been issued to the KGB's Morkrie Delia agents," Krio declared. "It's similar to the old MVD cyanide-gas gun used by SMERSH assassins. However, this tube contains an aerosol version of the Proteus Enzyme. One whiff and you're infected. You won't feel any different at first, but a few days later you'll suffer from stomach cramps. You'll become nauseous. You won't be able to defecate or urinate. You may go to a hospital, but they won't be able to help. . . ."

"Put that away," Kostov ordered. "We can't allow these two men to live for several days after what they've heard in this room. Besides, they deserve the professional consideration of a quick and dignified death.''

The colonel turned to Captain Vitosho and uttered a curt command in Bulgarian. Vitosho nodded. He stepped forward and aimed his Makarov pistol at Rafael Encizo's head. The cold steel muzzle pressed against the Cuban's temple.

Encizo's facial muscles tensed, but his eyes revealed stubborn defiance, not fear. Vitosho's finger slowly squeezed the trigger....

18

Encizo suddenly pivoted in his chair. He jerked his head away from the pistol and thrust the heel of his left hand into Vitosho's wrist. The Makarov roared and blasted a harmless round into the ceiling.

The Cuban's right hand whipped out to seize the pistol. Light flashed on the steel handcuffs that dangled from his wrist. He twisted the Makarov hard. Bone snapped. Vitosho howled. His finger had been caught in the trigger guard.

Encizo pulled the Makarov from the Bulgarian's grasp and quickly swung a backhand sweep at Vitosho's face. The empty handcuff manacle struck the captain's cheekbone, and Vitosho staggered backward from the blow.

Everyone in the room was startled by Encizo's unexpected actions. Unaccustomed to combat, Dimitri Krio stood dumbfounded, his mouth open in amazement. The two terrorist sentries, inexperienced and poorly trained, were even less prepared. They raised their weapons but hesitated, fearful of shooting Vitosho.

Colonel Kostov was a professional. He immediately reached for a Makarov pistol in a holster at the small of his back. However, Gary Manning was also a pro, and his youthful reflexes were faster than the Bulgarian's.

The Canadian bolted from his chair and quickly rammed the top of his hard skull into Krio's chest. The head butt propelled Krio backward into Kostov before the colonel could draw his Makarov. Both men stumbled into a wall.

One of the terrorists had switched the safety selector of his Czech Model 61 submachine gun to semiautomatic. He prepared to aim the weapon at Encizo. Manning's hands were still cuffed behind his back, but his feet were not bound. He suddenly kicked the machine pistol out of the guard's fingers.

The startled terrorist snarled and reached for Manning's throat. The Canadian turned sharply and lunged his right buttock and hip between the man's splayed legs. A choking gasp erupted from the terrorist's throat as he folded in agony.

Manning promptly slammed a knee under his opponent's jaw. The terrorist crashed to the floor, unconscious, but the other sentry swung his AK-47 at the Canadian. Encizo triggered the Makarov he had taken from Vitosho. A 9mm slug shattered skull bone and ripped through the terrorist's brain.

Two more members of the local goon squad burst into the room. Kostov aimed his Makarov at the Cuban. Vitosho had drawn a bayonet from its belt scabbard and prepared to lunge. Then everyone froze when they saw Encizo point his pistol at the gas canister on the floor.

"Go ahead," the Cuban invited, "kill me. But you'd better hope I don't manage to squeeze this trigger, or you'll all get a lethal dose of the Proteus Enzyme."

"Hold your fire!" Kostov ordered. He repeated

the command in three languages to be certain everyone understood him.

"What kind of Houdini trick did you have up your sleeve to get out of those cuffs?" Manning asked as he shuffled over to his Cuban partner.

"Not up my sleeve," Encizo replied with a grin, but he still aimed the Makarov at the canister. "I had a handcuff key taped to the inside of my belt at the small of my back. It's an old cop trick. If a hood gets the drop on a policeman and uses his own cuffs on him, the cop can use the hidden key to free himself."

"Sure glad your key fit the cuffs," Manning commented. "What did you do with it?"

"The key is on the chair," Encizo answered. "Okay, Kostov. Put down your weapon and tell everybody else to do likewise."

"He's bluffing," Krio declared.

"No," Kostov corrected. "Men who have nothing to lose have no reason to bluff about death."

Vitosho returned his bayonet to its sheath. He smiled despite the gash on his cheek and nodded respectfully at the Cuban. The captain then turned and marched out the door.

"I won't tell you again, Colonel," Encizo warned.

Kostov tossed his pistol onto the sofa and ordered the others to leave. The terrorists retreated from the building. Only the Phoenix Force pair, Kostov, Krio and the unconscious sentry remained.

"I told you just to make them lay down their arms," Encizo said. "I didn't say they were supposed to leave."

"You don't need them." Kostov shrugged.

After considerable effort and physical contortion,

Manning managed to get the handcuff key from the chair. He freed himself and gathered up the dead-man's Kalashnikov. "Order your boys to bring in another gas canister," the Canadian demanded. "And don't be cute this time, Kostov. Like you said, we've got nothing to lose."

Kostov shouted to the terrorists outside. A skinny female barbarian soon hauled a second tank across the threshold. Manning noticed she was unarmed except for a sheath knife on her belt. The Canadian gestured for her to give him the canister. She obeyed.

"Get her out of here," Manning ordered.

Kostov told the woman to leave. She walked to the door and turned to glare at Manning. The woman spat on the floor with contempt.

"Same to you, bitch," the Canadian muttered as he watched her leave. Manning slipped his arms through the straps of the canister harness.

"You have a plan, amigo?" Encizo asked, still aiming his pistol at the tank on the floor.

"I figure the dipshits outside will be reluctant to shoot at us if we're both carrying a tankful of killer enzyme," Manning explained, buckling the harness belt around his waist.

"Especially if we also have Kostov and Krio for hostages," Encizo added with a smile. "Sounds like the best plan possible under the circumstances."

"Using us for shields won't work," Kostov warned. "All of us are expendable. Our mission comes first."

"Of course," Encizo agreed as he picked up the first tank and slid into its harness. "But I suspect the folks outside won't risk killing you two unless they have to. My guess is they respect your leadership, Colonel . . . to say nothing of Krio's money.''

"Besides," Manning remarked. "Nobody wants to die of malnutrition. They won't want to risk puncturing one of these tanks with a bullet."

The Cuban gathered up the discarded Czech M-61 machine pistol. He was familiar with the Skorpion subgun, which was a favorite weapon of European terrorists. Encizo heard the stunned guard groan as he began to recover consciousness. The Cuban kicked him behind the ear to put him to sleep again.

"Face the wall," Manning told Krio and Kostov, gesturing with the AK-47.

The Canadian handcuffed their wrists at the small of their backs. He quickly frisked the pair, paying special attention to the Bulgarian agent. He was glad he did. Kostov had a variation of the hidden-key trick. Manning found a thin hacksaw blade taped to the inside of Kostov's belt.

"Neither of the guards has any spare magazines for these weapons," Encizo stated as he gathered up Kostov's Makarov from the sofa. "We'd better hurry, Gary. That son of a bitch Vitosho is probably planning a reception for us by now."

Manning took Krio's spray tube of the enzyme and slipped it into his own pocket. "Proteus Number Five, eh?" the Canadian said dryly. "We need transportation, Krio. Your people are loading tanks onto boats. The yacht harbor is too far away, so you must have some vessels docked on this side of the island. Right?"

"There is another harbor less than five hundred meters from here," Krio confirmed. "But you'll never make it."

"Then neither will you, fella," Manning warned.

CAPTAIN IGOR VITOSHO clenched his teeth and cursed softly as he bound his broken index finger to the next digit. A crude splint, but it would have to do. Vitosho accepted the pain as part of his punishment for being taken off guard by the Cuban.

The young Bulgarian had been born in 1956. The Soviet Union had ruled his country for more than a decade. Igor was an intelligent youth and a natural athlete. In a Communist state, this made him the ideal choice for an elite military corps.

Raised on extremist propaganda and exposed only to the "Gospel of Saint Marx," Vitosho felt obligated to be a good citizen and to obey the state. He was selected for the Bulgarian parachute corps. He excelled in languages, weapons' use, military tactics and close-quarters combat. Vitosho was honored to serve the cause of his Communist master, and he was especially pleased to be the second-in-command under the great war hero Colonel Nikolai Kostov.

But he had failed Kostov. Vitosho blamed himself for allowing the two commandos to turn tables on their captors. He vowed to rectify this error and prove himself worthy of the rank of an officer of an elite fighting unit of the People's Republic of Bulgaria.

Vitosho had rapidly prepared his troops to deal with the capitalist swine. He had trained the small army himself. They had been poor material for soldiers. Terrorists were usually undisciplined, unreliable in stress situations and mentally unbalanced. Yet Vitosho had found a handful of promising fighting men among this sorry stock. They would be enough to ensure the destruction of the Phoenix Force pair.

DIMITRI KRIO EMERGED from the officers' quarters first. He stumbled awkwardly across the threshold. Rafael Encizo was behind the Greek, prodding him with the muzzle of the Skorpion machine pistol. Kostov followed, escorted by Manning, armed with the AK-47.

Vitosho watched their progress from the cover of the concrete lab building. The soft dawn sun in a gold-and-lavender sky bathed the island with soft light. The Bulgarian captain grimly congratulated himself for correctly assuming the infiltrators' tactics. He had guessed they wanted the extra gas tank of the enzyme so both men could wear canisters on their backs while they used their hostages for shields.

The captain would not have been disappointed if his guess had been wrong.

Vitosho's troops could not simply shoot the two commandos without risking the release of the Proteus Enzyme. Besides, Vitosho wanted to rescue Colonel Kostov. Krio was a greedy pig and a traitor to his native Greece, but Kostov was a great Bulgarian patriot.

Vitosho hoped to avoid any shooting, although he had stationed marksmen on the rooftops of the lab building and the main barracks. The snipers were under strict orders not to open fire unless they had a clear head shot.

The Bulgarian waited tensely as he watched Manning, Encizo and their prisoners move along the side of the officers' billets. There was only one way to leave the island. The commandos would head for the harbor to steal a boat. Vitosho almost wished he believed in God, as he was tempted to pray. "A little farther," he whispered. "Just a little farther."

Encizo noticed a flash of light on a rooftop. A reflection against glass, he realized. A sniper with a scoped rifle. "Better keep your head down," the Cuban advised.

"I saw it," Manning assured him. "There are also terrorists lurking along the sides of the buildings. Might be some waiting right around the corner."

"Or on the..." Encizo began as he glanced up at the roof of the officers' billets.

He saw several figures poised on the edge. Backs arched, knees bent, they prepared to pounce on the Phoenix Force duo like a pack of hungry hyenas. Most of the terrorist ambushers held knives or hatchets in their fists.

With a bestial battle cry, the barbarians leaped from the roof and attacked.

19

"Shit!" Encizo exclaimed as he raised his Skorpion machine pistol and opened fire.

A spray of 7.65mm slugs slashed into two airborne figures. War whoops became shrieks of agony as their bodies convulsed in midair. Encizo stepped aside to let the corpses crash to earth.

Another attacker managed to avoid the stream of Skorpion projectiles. The terrorist collided with Encizo. The Czech subgun was knocked from the Cuban's hands as both men fell against the wall.

Encizo did not waste time grappling with the man. He rammed a knee into the terrorist's gut. The goon groaned and bent at the middle. Encizo seized his opponent's hair and drove the guy's face into the wall. Bone crunched, and the terrorist slid to the ground. A crimson smear marked his path along the wall.

Gary Manning had also been attacked by two assassins who leaped from the roof. He brought up his AK-47 and smashed the steel frame into a flying form. The blow sent the terrorist hurtling over Manning's head. The man fell to earth in a dazed, bloodied lump.

Another opponent landed beside Manning and grabbed the Kalashnikov with both hands. The Canadian hooked his left fist into the terrorist's face.

The guy's head danced from the punch, but he stubbornly held on to Manning's rifle.

Strong fingers seized the Canadian's hair from behind. A knife blade swung for Manning's throat. The Phoenix Force survivalist automatically recoiled from the slashing steel. He powered himself backward. The man clinging to Manning's back grunted when he smacked into the wall. The guy holding the AK-47 was towed forward.

Manning gasped in pain when the knife slit flesh. The blade cut a shallow furrow across the Canadian's chest, ripping through shirt and skin. Still holding on to the Kalashnikov with his right hand, Manning managed to pin the wrist behind the knife under his biceps.

He snapped his head back to butt the rear opponent in the face. Manning's left fist battered the front adversary's features. A hook punch, followed by a back fist and a quick jab stunned the terrorist. Then Manning released the Kalashnikov to seize the rear opponent's wrist with both hands.

The Canadian suddenly lunged forward. He pulled the rear attacker's knife arm forward to drive the blade into the front man's chest. One terrorist tumbled to the ground with the knife buried in his heart.

Manning thrust a back elbow stroke to the other man's jaw. The guy's head bounced back, and a projectile hit his exposed throat. Vertebrae shattered as the bullet passed through his neck.

Manning heard the harsh report of a rifle as blood fountained from the terrorist's bullet-torn throat. A sniper had missed his intended target and slain one of his own comrades, instead.

A hatchet-wielding killer charged Rafael Encizo, his weapon raised for a murderous swing intended to split the Cuban's skull. Encizo suddenly pivoted and turned his back to the assailant as he ducked his head. The terrorist gasped and froze before he could carry out the hatchet stroke, fearful of striking the gas canister on the Cuban's back.

The hatchetman did not get a chance to change tactics. Encizo heel-kicked the guy's genitals. The terrorist shrieked and dropped his ax to clutch both hands to his crushed manhood. The Cuban pulled a Makarov from his belt and whirled to chop the pistol into the side of his opponent's skull. Another member of Krio Island's terror army crumbled to the ground.

But the Phoenix Force warriors had little reason to rejoice. Both Krio and Kostov had taken advantage of the battle to flee for cover. Worse, a dozen terrorists had charged from the barracks and lab building.

The Cuban flicked off the safety catch of his Makarov and aimed the double-action Russian autoloader at the closest attacker. He fired two 9mm rounds into the fanatic's chest. The terrorist collapsed in a dying heap, but the others kept coming.

Fortunately the goon patrol was still afraid to shoot back because of the Proteus Enzyme. Encizo drew the other Makarov and fired both pistols at the advancing horde. Manning scooped up his AK-47 and blasted the terrorists with a salvo of full-auto destruction. Bodies twisted, convulsed and tumbled. Only three members of the kamikaze group survived to retreat back to shelter.

A sniper bullet scorched air inches from Encizo's ear. He instinctively ducked. Another slug kicked up dust between his feet. "They're going to try to cripple us," he shouted to Manning. "Shoot out our legs and move in for the kill!"

"Back inside!" the Canadian cried, firing a quick burst of 7.62mm rounds at the enemy to try to encourage them to stay down.

The Phoenix Force fighters retreated to the officers' quarters. A sniper slug splintered the doorway above Manning's head as he scrambled inside. Encizo followed and kicked the door shut. The shooting outside stopped abruptly.

A dull groan caught Manning's attention. The terrorist who had previously been left unconscious in the room had begun to recover. He started to rise to his feet, only to be knocked senseless by the Canadian's fist.

"Just not your day, fella," Manning muttered. "Hasn't been so great for us, either."

"Well," the Cuban said, panting hard. "It seemed like a good plan."

"Yeah." Manning nodded. "We'll have to come up with something else. We sure can't stay here for long."

"You were hit," Encizo said with concern when he noticed blood on his partner's shirtfront.

"Just a scratch," the Canadian assured him. "Would have been worse if the bastard had succeeded at trying to cut my throat."

"Any suggestions on how we can get out of this mess?" Encizo asked wearily.

"Maybe we can't," Manning replied simply.

"Well, none of us figured we'd live to a ripe old age doing this sort of work." The Cuban sighed. "But I hate to die without a fight."

"We've got one rifle, two pistols and damn little ammunition left," the Canadian stated. "How much of a fight can we give a small army?"

"We can still go down swinging," Encizo insisted.

"Or go out with a bang," Manning said as he slid out of the harness to the gas tank.

"What do you have in mind?" The Cuban frowned.

The Canadian unbuckled his belt and pulled it from his trousers. He unzipped the money compartment and removed a strip of C-4 plastic explosive.

"I can use this to explode the gas tanks," Manning explained. "That'll spew the Proteus Enzyme all over the island. Krio, Kostov and all their little helpers will be infected by the virus."

"And we'll be blown to bits." Encizo sighed.

"Yeah," his partner admitted. "But at least we'll die quickly—which beats hell out of wasting away from malnutrition. None of those bastards outside will live more than a week after we're dead."

"That might be long enough for them to carry out their mission," the Cuban remarked.

"They won't be able to complete all of it," Manning said, taking a fountain pen from his pocket. "And don't forget that the rest of Phoenix Force is still on the job in Athens."

"We really don't have many options left," Encizo reluctantly agreed.

"That's a fact," the Canadian confirmed as he dismantled the pen to extract a pencil detonator. "Give me your tank, as well...."

A horrible sound erupted. A whoosh of air and a roar was followed by a fierce wave of heat. Flame burst through the walls and glass exploded from the windows. Manning and Encizo fell to the floor. Within seconds they were surrounded by intense flames and heat, made worse by a nauseating chemical odor.

"Flamethrowers!" Manning exclaimed. "They're using flamethrowers to destroy the enzyme before it can spread."

"And us with it," the Cuban added as the blaze increased rapidly.

20

The officers' lounge became a raging inferno. Encizo and Manning felt as if they were inside a pressure cooker.

The Canadian handed his AK-47 to Encizo. "Move," he rasped, gathering up the C-4 in one hand and the gas tank in the other. "Before this whole place burns."

Both men scrambled to the next doorway. Flames danced in their path. Burning debris fell from walls and ceiling. Smoke clogged their nostrils and slithered through their mouths and into their lungs in deadly snakes of vapor.

None of these obstacles stopped the Phoenix Force pair. They burst into a narrow corridor. Encizo turned to the closest door and smashed its lock with a well-placed kick. They entered a small room, with a bunk, footlocker and small metal desk its only furniture.

Heat had already shattered a window. Flame licked the sill, and the blaze began to spread along the walls.

Manning tore a chunk of C-4 from the strip. He judged the weight as he rolled it into a tiny ball. "Got about fifty or sixty grams here," he declared, slipping into the harness of the gas tank once again. "More than enough."

"What—" Encizo began. But smoke caught in his throat before he could finish the sentence.

"Blow the wall," Manning told him hoarsely as he inserted the pencil detonator into the C-4 sphere.

The Canadian demolitions expert moved to the wall by the bunk. Manning's head seemed to wobble loosely on the stem of his neck. The room whirled before him as he fell against the cot.

Lack of oxygen, his dizzy brain realized. The fire was burning it up rapidly. He knelt by the wall and placed the explosives in a corner. Tears fogged his eyes. Manning blinked to clear them well enough to see the dial setting of the detonator.

"Gary!" Encizo shouted as the blaze continued to increase. Dense smoke nearly blinded the Cuban. "For Christ's sake, hurry!"

Manning set the timer. He was not certain how many seconds he had selected. Less than ten, he guessed. The Canadian tried to rise. His legs buckled, and he tumbled onto the cot.

Encizo grabbed Manning and pulled him across the mattress. The Cuban helped Manning to his feet. Both men staggered across the threshold into the corridor.

The explosion shook the building. Chunks of wood, plaster dust and pieces of flaming, shredded mattress spewed from the doorway. The Phoenix Force duo waited for the debris to settle before they ventured back into the room.

Twisted metal and burning wreckage littered the floor. A large portion of the wall had been blown away. Sunlight poured through the gap like a ray of hope from heaven.

They headed for the hole. Encizo had left the AK-47 in his desperation to save Manning, and now the Russian rifle was buried under the debris. The Cuban handed a Makarov to the demo expert as they shuffled to the gap.

The pair plunged outside. They pulled the gas tanks loose as they staggered forward. All they needed was a couple of seconds to puncture the canisters with bullets before the terrorists gunned them down. Manning and Encizo prepared to confront the enemy for the last time.

Suddenly the metallic thunder of machine-gun fire pierced the ringing inside their ears, and an enormous shadow flashed across the ground as if a giant eagle swooped overhead. They glanced up to see the underbelly of a helicopter pass.

"My God," Manning whispered in disbelief when he looked down at the enemy corpses sprawled across the parade field.

THE RAID HAD BEGUN before dawn. Colonel Katzenelenbogen had planned the assault based on information given by Theo Xerxes. Calvin James, David McCarter and Manos Draco advised the Israeli on the finer points of a two-prong attack plan.

Katz, Nikkos Papadopoulos and a dozen Greek paratroopers disguised as fishermen had headed for the island aboard an old trawler. Uniformed security guards saw the fishing vessel approach. The sentries met the boat as it pulled into the yacht harbor next to the *Argo*.

"This is private property," a guard called through a bullhorn. "We must order you to leave immediately."

"One of our crew was attacked by a shark," Papadopoulos shouted back. "The fish bit off most of his
arm. The poor fellow has gone into shock and needs
medical attention."

"Head for the mainland," the sentry persisted.
"The coastal patrol will help you. You'll get nothing
but trouble from us."

"You chaps are the blokes lookin' for trouble,"
the Greek declared in his cockney-flavored English.
"And you'll bloody well get it."

Paratroopers opened fire with silencer-equipped
G-3 assault rifles. Manufactured by the Hellenic
Arms Industry, the Greek G-3 was modeled after the
Heckler & Koch rifle produced in West Germany.
The weapons certainly performed well enough in the
hands of the paratroopers. Only one enemy guard
lived long enough to scream before a 7.62mm slug
silenced him forever.

Katz, Papadopoulos and eight Greek commandos
leaped to the pier to encounter Krio's security men
who ran forward to investigate the cry of their dying
comrade. Most of the guard force had already been
called in to reinforce the terrorists on the opposite
side of the island. The security that remained at the
yacht harbor was minimal.

Only half a dozen guards confronted Katz's assault
team. Armed with just service pistols, the sentries
were no match for the commandos with their full-
auto firepower. However, the guards were either very
brave or very stupid. They aimed their handguns at
the invaders.

The Israeli freedom fighter burned three opponents in the flash of an eyelash. Nine-millimeter

rounds hissed through a foot-long sound suppressor attached to the muzzle of Katz's Uzi machine gun. The sentries hardly lived long enough to know what hit them.

Nikkos blasted another uniformed flunky with a silenced Sumak-9 submachine gun. The paratroopers took out the last two guards. So far things were going well. Katz was pleased to note that none of his men had even been scratched.

Katzenelenbogen ran toward the mansion. The rest of the team followed. The younger commandos were surprised to discover they had trouble keeping up with the Israeli warrior. Although middle-aged, ten pounds overweight and a smoker who averaged half a pack a day, Katz was still capable of surprising bursts of speed.

But like an old lion, he could not sustain a fast pace very long. Yet for a few vital minutes he became a whirlwind of muscle, teeth and claws.

A pair of uniformed figures emerged from the front door of the mansion. They pointed .45-caliber M-3 subguns at the strike force. Katz triggered his Uzi before either man could fire his grease gun. A volley of parabellum hailstones chewed through flesh to shatter bone and demolish vital organs.

The guards fell. Papadopoulos quickly lobbed an M-26 hand grenade through the open doorway. Katz and his men hit the pavement. The explosion blasted glass and framework from two windows. The front door dangled awkwardly on a single broken hinge.

Katz charged inside first. The hallway was littered with shattered pottery, plaster and fragments of three more slain sentries. However, two of Krio's men had merely been knocked down by the grenade blast.

Milo, Krio's personal valet, clamped a hand to the side of his head. He had suffered a ruptured eardrum during the explosion. The other gunman, dressed in a white dinner jacket, reached for a double-barreled shotgun.

The Uzi rasped harshly. A trio of 9mm slugs tore into the shotgunner's chest. The schmuck's body slid across the tile floor to the pedestal at the base of the staircase. Milo rose to one knee and reached for a pistol under his white jacket.

Katz closed the distance with two fast strides. Milo managed to draw his Yugoslavian M-57 automatic. The steel hooks of the Israeli's prosthesis snapped shut around the hand holding the pistol.

The Phoenix Force veteran exerted pressure. Milo screamed as bones in his fingers cracked and snapped. Katz's left hand swung like an ax to chop the gunman in the base of the neck. Milo slumped unconscious. The Israeli kicked the M-57 pistol away from the mangled, bloodied glob that had formerly been Milo's hand.

"Bleedin' hell, mate," Nikkos Papadopoulos declared as he entered the hallway. "You didn't leave much for the rest of us blokes to do."

"Don't be too certain about that," the Israeli replied. "We don't know what sort of surprises the enemy might have waiting for us in the rest of the house."

Probably not much," the Greek intel agent commented. "But I'll tell the lads to be careful. 'Course, the real fight is goin' on at the other side of the bleedin' island."

"Yes," Katz said with a sigh. "I know."

21

The second assault unit involved in the siege on Krio Island came from the skies. Two Bell UH-1D helicopters and an AC-130A gunship armed with 20mm Gatling guns swooped down on the terrorist camp. Their first pass had been simply a quick recon of the area.

"Looks like your friends started without us," Manos Draco remarked to Calvin James.

"I just hope they're still alive," James replied grimly as he stared down at the burning billets below.

James and Draco were inside the cabin of the gunship with fourteen Greek paratroopers, all qualified for frogman and UDT operations. They wore black wet suits, face masks, flippers and Emerson breathing apparatuses. The former Seal was glad the Greeks used the Emerson system. It indicated they knew what the hell they were doing.

"Tell the pilot to contact the chopper jockeys," James instructed. "Tell him to pass on the order *not* to hit that concrete building. It's the most solid structure down there, so that's probably where they're storing the chemicals. Don't blast the boats in the harbor, either. A couple of them have a lot of scuba tanks stacked on the decks."

"I don't understand why that worries you," Draco confessed.

"If you wanted to transport a deadly virus in a gaseous or liquid form," James answered, "what better way than carrying it in tanks disguised as scuba gear?"

"Good point." The Greek intel agent nodded.

"Everything else is pretty much open season," the black warrior told him. "We don't want to slaughter everybody down there, but if they want to play hard we'll have to play harder."

"What about your two friends?" Draco inquired.

"Stopping the terrorists is our main concern," James said bluntly. "If our pals are still alive, they'll try to stay that way. They've got enough sense to find cover and keep their heads down until this is over."

"Are all five of you so hard-nosed?" the Greek asked.

"Yeah," the Phoenix Force pro replied dryly. "But tell the pilots not to use the heavy artillery unless they absolutely have to. Let's try to convince those dudes to surrender without having to blow everything to hell."

"Which will reduce the risk to your friends, as well." Draco smiled. "Glad to see you're human after all."

"We're all human," James assured him. "That means none of us is bulletproof."

The aircraft circled around the terrorists. Several of the enemy troops opened fire on the choppers. They immediately regretted this action because the gunships retaliated. A tidal wave of 7.62mm bullets scythed away half a dozen troops. The rest fled for cover.

Gary Manning and Rafael Encizo emerged from the burning billets a few seconds later.

The two Bell whirlybirds completed a revolution beyond the shoreline, then headed back for the terrorist stronghold, ready for action. A voice, amplified by a megaphone, ordered the enemy to lay down their weapons and surrender.

The AC-130 required more space to maneuver. As it flew over the Mediterranean and headed back to Krio Island, the gunship gradually descended and slowed slightly.

"The pilot says we're roughly twenty meters over the water," Draco announced.

"That's about seventy feet, right?" James asked as he checked the large, thick rubber bag hooked to his weight belt. "That's a long jump without a chute."

"The pilot says he doesn't want to get any lower because he'll need to ascend and increase speed rapidly," the one-eyed Greek explained.

"Well, I guess he knows his business," the Phoenix fighter remarked.

"I haven't jumped out of a plane for years." Draco frowned. "Rather hoped I wouldn't have to do it again."

"You don't have to come along," James told him.

"You might need a translator." The Greek intel agent sighed. "But let's go before I lose my nerve, eh?"

James jumped from the cabin door. He kept his finned feet close together and raised his arms overhead. The Phoenix Force commando hit the surface and knifed through the water. The impact was a nasty jolt, but not really painful. Somewhat like falling out of bed and being jarred awake.

On rising to the surface, the black warrior immediately slipped his face mask into position. He paddled gently in the water and waited for the rest of the team. Manos Draco leaped into the sea next. The Greek intel agent may have hated to jump from planes, but he handled himself well underwater. One by one the paratroopers jumped into the drink.

The team waited until the last man hit the water to avoid someone landing on another diver. They exchanged nods to confirm everyone was all right. Calvin James held his right arm over head and pointed toward the island. The men recognized the signal to advance and nodded in reply.

THE AMPLIFIED VOICES from the gunships repeated the order in Greek, Bulgarian, Russian and English for the terrorists to surrender. The enemy did not seem to care what language was used. They were determined to disobey the command.

Numerous terrorists fired at the aircraft with assault rifles, but they were hardly a match for the choppers' mounted machine guns. Those who failed to find adequate cover were cut down by the gunships' merciless rain of copper-jacketed projectiles.

Manning and Encizo adopted a prone position close to the burning building. They stayed down until the choppers made their second pass before they removed the canisters of Proteus Enzyme. The pair no longer intended to release the virus, and they did not want a stray bullet to puncture the tanks. They hurled the canisters back into the billets to allow the blaze to destroy the enzyme.

The skinny female terrorist spotted Manning and

Encizo. She aimed a Soviet-made Stechkin machine pistol at the pair. Although fifty yards away, she opened fire with the weapon on full-auto. Had she used the semiauto mode, she might have hit the Phoenix Force fighters, but the Stechkin's full-auto range was only half what she required of it.

Nine-millimeter slugs ripped into the ground in front of Manning and Encizo. The Cuban raised his Makarov in a two-hand Weaver's grip and squeezed off three double-action rounds. Two 9mm slugs found flesh. The woman tumbled to the ground with a bullet in each breast.

Manning scooped up an AKMS assault rifle that had been discarded by its slain owner and set the selector switch to full-auto.

"Gary!" Encizo shouted as he pointed to a trio of terrorists positioned by the concrete lab building.

The Canadian saw the reason for his partner's concern. The terror troops were armed with two Russian RP-6 rocket launchers that would be capable of blasting a gunship from the sky with a single round. Manning brought the metal stock of the AKMS to his shoulder, snap-aimed and fired.

The terrorists spun and quivered as 7.62mm slugs punched through their bodies. The enemy troops crumbled against the thick steel door of the building. Manning hit them with a second volley of AKMS missiles to be certain they never got up again.

Most of the terrorists had fled to the main barracks, where extra ammunition and more effective weapons were stored. Two bold fanatics emerged from the building to set up a Soviet PKM machine gun mounted on a convertible tripod, adjusted to fire at aircraft. They were still fumbling with the weapon when the AC-130 returned.

The big gunship opened fire with her 20mm Gatlings. The terrorist machine gunners were literally torn apart by large-caliber slugs. What was left of the corpses could have been mistaken for the victims of an ax murderer.

SEVERAL TERRORISTS HAD NOTICED that the boats in the harbor had not been fired on by the gunships. Nine zealots, more concerned with survival than radical politics, bolted for the pier and climbed on board a pair of fishing trawlers.

Calvin James and his frogman team were waiting for them. The commando had removed his tank, flippers and weight belt. He had also removed his Smith & Wesson M-76 from its waterproof bag. The rest of the team were armed with either Sumak-9 submachine guns or M3A1 .45 grease guns.

"Throw your guns in the water and surrender!" Draco shouted in Greek.

The terrorists swung their weapons toward the sound of the intel man's voice. They did not get a second chance to surrender. James and his men opened fire.

It could hardly be called a battle. The terrorists were outnumbered almost two to one. Their opponents were better trained and more experienced. James and his men had also had ample time to position themselves behind the best cover available on the trawlers.

The assault force blasted several terrorists over the transom. Bodies splashed into the water and tumbled over handrails to crash to the pier. James noticed two enemy troops dash up the rungs of a ladder to the fly bridge of one of the vessels. The black bad ass hit the pair with a burst of 9mm messengers of destruction. A terrorist screamed and collapsed against the helm seat, while his comrade's bullet-riddled body slid down the ladder to the deck below.

"Draco!" James called out. "Order half the men to stay with the boats to guard them. The rest—"

A sudden movement caused James to whirl and face the fly bridge. The wounded terrorist had hauled himself upright and aimed a Skorpion machine pistol at the black man. James raised his S&W although he realized it was too late.

Suddenly the terrorist convulsed in agony. He arched his back and triggered the Czech blaster, firing a volley of bullets into the sky. Then the man stumbled over the lip of the fly bridge and belly flopped on the deck below. The haft of a diver's knife jutted from between his shoulder blades.

Manos Draco appeared on the fly bridge. Calvin James gave him a thumbs-up salute of thanks. The one-eyed Greek smiled and held up a hand with index finger and thumb together to reply, "Okay."

THE TERRORIST FORCES had suffered terrible casualties. Forty-six of them lay dead or dying. Many of the survivors had been wounded by stray bullets or flying shrapnel.

Colonel Nikolai Kostov decided there was only one logical choice of action left. The Bulgarian walked to the center of the parade field and raised his empty hands overhead. The remaining members of the terrorist army followed his example. Even Dimitri Krio reluctantly accepted defeat.

"My God," Gary Manning remarked as he threw down the AKMS to avoid being mistaken as a stubborn terrorist gunman. "We were ready to die a few minutes ago. Now we're not only still alive, we've won."

"We 'beat the clock,' as McCarter would say." Rafael Encizo smiled weakly. "Without a minute to spare."

The Cuban glanced toward the concrete lab building. A figure dressed in a white smock lay sprawled across the corpses of the terrorists Manning had gunned down during the firefight. The steel door stood open as a tall, powerful figure darted inside.

"*¡Mierda!*" Encizo exclaimed as he broke into a full run for the building. He drew the Makarov as he ran.

Encizo barely glimpsed the face of the man in white, but he recognized Dr. Chekov. The Russian's eyes stared lifelessly at the sky above. His throat had been slit open from one ear to the other.

Encizo guessed the identity of Chekov's assassin. His suspicion was confirmed when he spotted the hard Nordic features of Igor Vitosho. The Bulgarian captain peered out from the doorway. Blood dripped from the blade of a bayonet in his fist.

The Cuban fired his Makarov. A 9mm slug ricocheted against the doorway. Vitosho recoiled and moved away from the entrance. The steel door began to swing shut.

Encizo leaped forward and dived through the opening. He landed in an awkward shoulder roll that carried him into the field desk in the foyer. A boot lashed out, kicking the Makarov from the Cuban's hand.

Vitosho towered over Encizo, bayonet held in an underhand grip in his left fist. The Bulgarian fell on his opponent, planning to pin Encizo to the floor and plunge the knife between the Cuban's ribs.

The Phoenix Force veteran raised both feet to deliver a powerful kick that sent Vitosho hurtling across the room. Encizo sprang to his feet as the Bulgarian adopted a knife-fighter's stance. He arched his back and held the bayonet low.

Encizo was a skilled knife artist himself. He knew when a man was experienced with a blade and Vitosho did not appear to be a novice. The Cuban shuffled his feet into the T-*dachi* position as he held his open hands poised like the claws of an eagle.

Vitosho feinted a thrust, then tossed the bayonet to his right hand and lunged from a different direction. Encizo sidestepped away from the flashing blade and tried to parry his opponent's wrist with the heel of his left palm.

The Bulgarian was quick. He suddenly altered his attack and attempted a cross-body slash. Encizo's *teshio* stroke hit the captain's hand. Vitosho hissed painfully when the blow smashed into his already-broken finger. The bayonet clattered to the floor.

Vitosho snarled a *kiai* and suddenly lashed a karate side kick to Encizo's chest. The Cuban crashed backward into a wall. The Bulgarian slashed a deadly *shuto* stroke for his opponent's throat. Encizo's crossed wrists formed an X block to check the captain's hand chop.

Encizo seized his adversary's forearm and twisted it forcibly. He snap-kicked Vitosho in the abdomen and followed with a simple ankle-trip takedown. A fundamental judo move, it worked well enough to throw Vitosho to the floor.

The captain landed on his back with a surprised grunt. Encizo immediately bent his right knee and dropped forward with all his weight behind the punishing blow that hit Vitosho squarely in the solar plexus. The Bulgarian's breath spewed from his lungs and his body went limp.

Encizo chopped the side of his hand into Vitosho's neck muscle to be certain his opponent was unconscious. The Cuban raised his hand to strike again, but he sighed and lowered his arm. "You've had enough, Captain," Encizo said wearily. "We've all had enough."

The electrical hum of the door opening drew his attention to the entrance. Colonel Kostov stood at the threshold. Yakov Katzenelenbogen was behind the Bulgarian, his Uzi pointed at Kostov's head.

"Ah, amigo." Encizo smiled. "Am I glad to see you."

"The colonel offered to work the combination to the control panel," Katz stated. "I just wanted to make certain he got all the numbers right. Gary was ready to blow the door open with a strip of C-4. You know how he is about demolitions."

"How'd the raid turn out?" Encizo asked as he dragged Vitosho to the door.

"A couple of Greek paratroopers received minor shrapnel wounds," the Israeli announced. "Otherwise we didn't suffer a single casualty. The entire island is under our control now."

"Did you kill him?" Kostov inquired, referring to the limp figure of Igor Vitosho.

"No," Encizo replied. "Although he would have killed all of us if he'd gotten to the lab and released the enzyme."

"The captain was trying to complete his mission." Kostov sighed. "I imagine he thinks I'm a traitor for surrendering, but the battle was already lost. There was nothing to be gained by more killing."

"There wouldn't have been any killing if your masters in the KGB hadn't started this fight," the Cuban told him.

"Perhaps." The Bulgarian nodded. "What are you going to do with us, now that you've caught us?"

"That's up to the Greek authorities," Katz answered. "I imagine you and Vitosho will be tried for espionage. Probably hold you until they can arrange to trade you for a prisoner from our side who is currently held captive behind the iron curtain. You know how this business works."

"You could kill me," Kostov remarked.

"We'd rather you take a message to the KGB," Katz stated. "Tell them not to mistake mercy for weakness. If they start a fight, we'll finish it. If they have any more schemes like the Proteus Enzyme plot, they'd better cancel their plans."

"Because we'll be waiting to kick their ass if they don't," Encizo added bluntly.

22

The Greek paratroopers expertly frisked the terrorists and bound their hands behind their backs with riot cuffs. Calvin James personally guarded Dimitri Krio.

The Greek tycoon did not seem concerned about the situation. "My friends in parliament won't let me go to prison, you know," Krio stated.

"You think your cronies at city hall will bail your ass out when they find out you've been charged with treason?" James sneered. "No crooked politician is gonna take a risk like that, dude."

"I'll stand trial," Krio agreed. "But I'll be released. Probably have to leave Greece, of course. But a man with my wealth and influence will certainly be welcomed elsewhere. South America, for example."

"You may be right, Krio," Gary Manning declared as he approached. "But you're not going to stand trial."

"Oh?" Krio chuckled. "So the American CIA wants to make a deal? Very well, I'll listen."

"We're not CIA," the Canadian told him. "And there will be no deal. We can almost excuse the Bulgarians. After all, they were acting under orders. They've got some pretty warped notions about their country due to the KGB, but at least they thought they were acting in the best interests of their country.''

Manning drew a Makarov automatic from his belt. Krio stiffened, and Calvin James raised his eyebrows in surprise. The Greek relaxed a bit when he noticed Manning's arm dangled loosely at his side, pointing the pistol at the ground.

"But you don't have an excuse, Krio," the Canadian continued. "Not even a weak one. You were part of this vicious conspiracy for purely selfish reasons. That makes your involvement unforgivable."

"What are you going to do?" Krio asked nervously. "Kill me?"

"Not exactly," Manning replied as he reached into a pocket with his other hand. "You don't deserve a nice quick execution."

The roar of a gunshot startled everyone in the area. Katz and Encizo rushed to the scene, escorting Kostov at gunpoint. Krio was shrieking in agony. Smoke curled from the muzzle of Manning's pistol.

"Jesus, Gary," James rasped.

The Canadian had shot Krio in the foot.

Before the corrupt Greek could fall, Manning's left hand thrust a metal tube between Krio's teeth. He sprayed a mist into the tycoon's open mouth. Krio landed on his backside, moaning and sobbing as he stared at the bloodied hole in the instep of his left shoe.

"Krio," Manning said, waving the lettle spray can in his hand. "This is your little tube of Proteus breath freshener. Remember?"

The Greek's eyes swelled in horror. His mouth remained open, but terror overwhelmed pain. It froze his vocal cords in an icy death grip.

"That's right, Krio," Manning remarked dryly. "Hope you enjoy malnutrition, you bastard."

"Bravo, Gary," Encizo said with heartfelt satisfaction.

"We'd better get out of here," Katz declared. "The real battle is waiting for us back in Athens."

"What do you mean?" the Cuban asked.

"McCarter is recovering from a minor wound, so we didn't bring him on the raid," Katz answered. "He's going to be furious when we tell him what he missed."

"WE'VE GOT the Proteus Enzyme, Mr. Premier." The President of the United States spoke into the red phone. It was not a telephone but a transatlantic communications device, a direct line to Moscow. The President sat alone in a tiny soundproof room with the contraption. At one time a Russian interpreter had to assist the President on the hot line. Technology now improved security. The premier's reply was translated into English by a language computer hooked up to the red phone.

"What is the Proteus Enzyme, Mr. President?" the premier asked.

"You already know about Proteus. Let's not play games, sir. Certainly you've been informed about what happened at Krio Island yesterday."

"Dreadful business," the premier stated. "Apparently Dimitri Krio was harboring a large number of international terrorists. For some reason a battle erupted and the Greek military had to take rather drastic action. According to reports, Krio was seriously wounded. He's in a hospital in critical condition and not expected to recover.''

"That's the official version," the President confirmed. "The Greeks are certainly happy with it. They're describing the incident as their Grenada.''

"How droll.''

"But you and I know the truth, Mr. Premier. We've both got Proteus now. The formula is in the hands of American scientists, as well as the Russians.''

"Congratulations," the Soviet boss said. "I see you've got some very good clandestine people.''

"The best, Mr. Premier. The very best.''

"And you're calling to let us know if we use Proteus, you're prepared to retaliate with it.'' The Premier was not asking a question.

"The balance of power, Mr. Premier," the President confirmed.

"I understand," the premier assured him. "Are we going to have to discuss this business at the United Nations?''

"That could be embarrassing for both of us. You don't want to admit you developed Proteus, and we don't want to talk about reproducing it.''

"I appreciate your tact, Mr. President.''

"So you want to keep a lid on Proteus?''

"Obviously. Moscow has more to fear from publicity than Washington. We need not discuss Proteus again.''

"If the subject comes up again," the President explained, "we won't just discuss it on the phone. I trust you understand.''

"Of course. We all act in our own best interests. I believe that concludes our business for now, Mr. President."

"I agree, Mr. Premier."

"Oh, you might tell those very special people of yours that I'm quite impressed by their work. Some of my people hope to meet them someday. . .professionally."

"They'll be ready, should that occur."

"It will, Mr. President. Sooner or later. It will."

"Good day, Mr. Premier."

"A good day to you, sir."

The President ended transmission.

The Gar Wilson Forum

Throughout history, assassination has been used by the lunatic fringe as an instrument of self-styled political change. The word "assassin" itself derives from an Arabic word meaning "hashish eaters," as it was believed that the politico-religious Islamic sect who became known as the Assassins took hashish before undertaking their barbarous acts of terrorism.

This cancerous activity, that in the end must be perceived as an act of madness and desperation, is no stranger to the United States. The names Lincoln, Garfield and Kennedy remind us just how vulnerable our elected leaders are to the homicidal whims of the politically and emotionally unbalanced. Gerald Ford faced two assassination attempts, and Ronald Reagan was the target of an assassin's bullet in 1983.

But we continue to insist that our politicians be accessible to us, and that the day-to-day details of their lives be made into public property. Because we demand that our elected and chosen leaders reveal their private and public lives through the press, on radio and on television, shouldn't we, as citizens, shoulder some of the responsibility when a gun-wielding fanatic takes murderous advantage of our demands to carry out an ill-conceived plan of cold-blooded murder? This responsibility is part of the price of democracy.

Gar

PHOENIX FORCE

#14 Phoenix in Flames

MORE GREAT ACTION
COMING SOON!

The Phoenix strike force blitzes into Turkey to confront
the Russian bear in an unfamiliar lair. The mission:
terminate a twisted KGB plan to destabilize the United
States from within by turning the American family home
into a hell zone.

Enlisting the aid of a West German GSG-9 antiterrorist
who has infiltrated the Turkish underworld, the five
combat-hardened veterans of the Force launch an
explosive assault aimed at the very heart of the
international terrorist network.

The firefight blazes, and only the Phoenix can rise from
the flames.

Watch for new Phoenix Force titles
wherever paperbacks are sold.

Mack Bolan's
PHOENIX FORCE
by Gar Wilson

Schooled in guerilla warfare, equipped with all the latest lethal hardware, Phoenix Force battles the powers of darkness in an endless crusade for freedom, justice and the rights of the individual. Follow the adventures of one of the legends of the genre. Phoenix Force is the free world's foreign legion!

"Gar Wilson is excellent! Raw action attacks the reader on every page."

—*Don Pendleton*

Phoenix Force titles are available wherever paperbacks are sold.

GOLD EAGLE

Nile Barrabas and the
Soldiers of Barrabas are the

SOBs

by Jack Hild

Nile Barrabas is a nervy son of a bitch who was the last American soldier out of Vietnam and the first man into a new kind of action. His warriors, called the Soldiers of Barrabas, have one very simple ambition: to do what the Marines can't or won't do. Join the Barrabas blitz! Each book hits new heights—this is brawling at its best!

"Nile Barrabas is one tough SOB himself.... A wealth of detail.... SOBs does the job!"

—*West Coast Review of Books*

#1 The Barrabas Run   #3 Butchers of Eden
#2 The Plains of Fire   #4 Gulag War

Available or coming soon
wherever paperbacks are sold.

JOIN FORCES WITH MACK BOLAN AND HIS NEW COMBAT TEAMS!

Mail this coupon today!